"I shall reward you, young Sahib, and your governor also, if he
will give me the shelter I ask."

THE SIGN OF FOUR

THE

SIGN OF FOUR

BY

A. CONAN DOYLE

AUTHOR OF

"A STUDY IN SCARLET," "THE REFUGEES," ETC.

APPLEWOOD BOOKS
BEDFORD, MASSACHUSETTS
1994

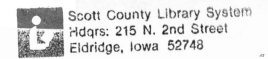
The Sign of Four was originally published in 1893 by J. B. Lippincott Company.

ISBN 1-55709-301-6

Thank you for purchasing an Applewood Book. Applewood Books reprints America's lively classics–books from the past that are still of interest to modern readers. For a free copy of our catalog, please write to Applewood Books, 18 North Road, Bedford, MA 01730.

10 9 8 7 6 5 4 3 2 1

Library of Congress Cataloging-in-Publication Data
Doyle, Arthur Conan, Sir, 1859-1930.
    The sign of four / by A. Conan Doyle.
        p.   cm.   – (The Library of Congress centennial best-seller series)
    "Author of 'A study in scarlet,' 'The refugees,' etc."
    "Republished in cooperation with the Library of Congress."
    ISBN 1-55709-301-6
    1. Holmes, Sherlock (Fictitious character)–Fiction.
    2. Private investigators–England–Fiction.   I. Title.
II. Title: Sign of 4.   III. Series.
PR4622.S44   1994
823'.8–dc20   93-50112
                                                      CIP

FOREWORD

The Library of Congress came into being almost two hundred years ago as a resource for the nation's legislature. Guided by the belief of Thomas Jefferson, its principal founder, that there is "no subject to which a Member of Congress may not have occasion to refer," it has grown from one room in the U.S. Capitol into the largest repository of recorded knowledge in the world. Today the Library holds in its collections more than 100 million items, of which more than 20 million are books. The wealth contained in this accumulation of volumes lies not only in the pages themselves but in the history they reveal—the attitudes and interests of the eras in which they were published and the lives of people who have been enlightened, entertained, and uplifted in reading them.

The Library of Congress "Centennial Bestsellers" series, which this volume inaugurates, is an expression of the Library's commitment to preserving and celebrating literature as a living force in the evolution of our nation. Drawn from diverse realms of both fiction and nonfiction, volumes in the series will allow voices from the literary past to speak anew, bringing their ideas, attitudes, judgments, and prejudices to an audience poised at a later vantage point in history.

Not all of the "Centennial Bestsellers" have had the staying power of *The Sign of Four*. But all reflect the era when they were read and discussed, and as such are not only valuable windows on our past but part of that vast and diverse sea of influences that have made our society what it is today. We are pleased to celebrate America's literary heritage by embarking with Applewood Books on this unique series.

—James H. Billington
The Librarian of Congress

IN THE COMPANY OF BOOKS
AN INTRODUCTION

*"It is a great thing to start life with a small number
of really good books which are your very own."*

Sir Arthur Conan Doyle published that thought in
Through the Magic Door, eleven years after publication of *The
Sign of Four*, a "ripping good" yarn featuring the foremost detective in all of crime literature—Sherlock Holmes. In the
America of 1893, enough people embraced this Holmes adventure as their very own to make *The Sign of Four* what would
today be termed a "bestseller"—a book which, for whatever reason, piques enough interest, provokes enough curiosity, creates
enough excitement to draw thousands of people to bookstores
to purchase the volume for their own leisurely consideration—
and perhaps for a lasting place upon their own bookshelves.

When *The Sign of Four* was published, no "Bestseller
List" existed in the United States. That would be created two
years later, in 1895, when *Bookman* magazine was founded in
this country and began listing each month in its back pages the
half-dozen bestselling books in various cities, based on sales
reports from bookstores. Yet scholars and bibliographers have
been able to create, from various records, lists of books that
were most popular in this country in its earlier years, and their
lists provide fascinating glimpses of the character and interests
of the reading public in America back to our earliest days.

In the seventeenth century John Bunyan's *Pilgrim's
Progress*, an enduring classic of world literature, was purchased
for many American homes—as was the first book by a woman
to become an American bestseller, *The Sovereignty and Goodness
of God: Together with the Faithfulness of His Promises Displayed;
Being a Narrative of the Captivity and Restauration of Mrs. Mary*

Rowlandson. The first of what came to be called the "Indian Captive narratives," Mrs. Rowlandson's informative if biased testimonial embodies one of the most persistently challenging aspects of the American experiment: the interaction—peaceful and otherwise—of different cultural groups as the American "commonwealth of cultures" continually reshapes itself.

The eighteenth century—marked on this continent by the intellectual and political ferment that resulted in the creation of the United States—saw publication in America of a burgeoning array of landmark pamphlets, broadsides, periodicals, and books—including works on morality by Cotton Mather and Jonathan Edwards, *The History of the Five Indian Nations* by Cadwallader Colden, *Poor Richard's Almanac* by the redoubtable Benjamin Franklin, and the *Grammatical Institute of the English Language* by Revolutionary War veteran Noah Webster, who passionately believed that Americans should have "a system of our own, in language as well as government." Other widely read books in this century included Flavius Josephus's *Antiquities of the Jews* and the phenomenally popular *Meditations and Contemplations* of devotional essayist James Hervey.

Uncle Tom's Cabin, or Life Among the Lowly by Harriet Beecher Stowe, a book that galvanized American political opinion in the years before the Civil War; *Struggling Upward and Other Works* by "rags-to-riches" storyteller Horatio Alger; *Little Women*, a "novel for young readers" by Louisa May Alcott that sounded, and continues to sound, strong chords in older readers as well; Wilkie Collins' *The Moonstone*—the first English detective novel; and *The Innocents Abroad*, Mark Twain's ferociously droll report on a trip to the Middle East and Mediterranean: all preceded *The Sign of Four* as nineteenth-century American bestsellers.

At the end of that century, the United States was continuing to grow rapidly into a mechanized and urbanized nation. Increases in public education, public libraries, and organizations and activities devoted to learning were creating a more cosmopolitan society. But growth and change are never painless.

The economic life of the country was affected by strikes and financial panics—including a worldwide depression that began in the spring of 1893. Antitrust legislation was passed to combat business monopolies, and a band of unemployed workers dubbed "Coxey's Army" marched on Washington, D.C., demanding jobs and changes in federal monetary policy. Nearly four million immigrants entered the U.S. during this decade, adding to the social ferment. In 1896 the U.S. Supreme Court, deciding *Plessy v. Ferguson*, strengthened racial segregation by affirming the doctrine of "separate but equal"—which would not be struck down until the 1950s. In 1895 Utah entered the Union and at the same time became the second state to give women the vote—one victory in a long struggle for woman suffrage that would not be over for another quarter-century.

In 1893, Madame Sarah Grand published *The Heavenly Twins*, a novel, largely forgotten today, which became a best-seller due to its author's belief in women's rights and her fictional presentation of hitherto taboo subjects. Robert Louis Stevenson's frightening tale of *Dr. Jekyll and Mr. Hyde* became a bestseller that year and has continued to fascinate readers with its contemplation of good and evil. And, of course, *The Sign of Four*, the story that, in its first appearance in *Lippincott's Monthly Magazine* three years earlier, introduced American readers to Sherlock Holmes, the detective whose logic finds the answers to even the most difficult problems, became a bestseller upon its publication in book form. Perhaps the clarity of thought and the incorruptibility of action that Holmes brings to every problem is what drew readers of one hundred years ago, as it attracts us today in a world that moves even faster and with ever more complexity.

Conan Doyle created Holmes out of the mysteries of his own imagination, of course, but part of that process was borrowing characteristics from real people he had encountered. One of these was Dr. Joseph Bell, a surgeon in Edinburgh, Scotland, where Doyle had studied medicine. Bell's formidable powers of deductive reasoning became Holmes's foremost characteristic.

Perhaps for that reason Bell took a keen interest in his fictional doppelganger, and in the literary abilities of Holmes's creator, which he noted in his introduction to a 1902 edition of *The Sign of Four*:

> Conan Doyle . . . has proved himself a born storyteller. He has had the wit to devise excellent plots, interesting complications; he tells them in honest Saxon-English with directness and pith; and, above all his other merits, his stories are absolutely free from padding. He knows how delicious brevity is, how everything tends to be too long, and he has given us stories that we can read at a sitting between dinner and coffee, and we have not a chance to forget the beginning before we reach the end.

Brevity, clarity, mystery, solution, crime, punishment: "Elementary," as Holmes would say.

The Center for the Book was created to remind people of the pleasures and influences of books. Appropriately, it is part of the Library of Congress, the nation's largest library and the world's premier repository of the intellectual wealth of the community of nations. We are pleased to bring these books, and the valuable window on the past they provide, to the renewed attention of readers.

John Y. Cole
Director
The Center for the Book in the Library of Congress

CONTENTS.

THE SIGN OF FOUR.

CHAPTER I.

THE SCIENCE OF DEDUCTION.

SHERLOCK HOLMES took his bottle from the corner of the mantelpiece, and his hypodermic syringe from its neat morocco case. With his long, white, nervous fingers he adjusted the delicate needle, and rolled back his left shirt-cuff. For some little time his eyes rested thoughtfully upon the sinewy forearm and wrist, all dotted and scarred with innumerable puncture-marks. Finally, he thrust the sharp point home, pressed down the tiny piston, and sank back into the velvet-lined arm-chair with a long sigh of satisfaction.

Three times a day for many months I had witnessed this performance, but custom had not reconciled my mind to it. On the contrary, from day to day I had become more irritable at the sight, and my conscience swelled nightly within me at the thought that I had lacked the courage to protest. Again and again I had registered a vow that I should deliver my soul upon the subject; but there was that in the cool, nonchalant air of my companion which made him the last man with whom one would care to take anything approaching to a liberty. His great powers, his masterly manner, and the experience which I had had of his many extraordinary qualities, all made me diffident and backward in crossing him.

Yet upon that afternoon, whether it was the Beaune which I had taken with my lunch, or the additional exasperation produced by the extreme deliberation of his manner, I suddenly felt that I could hold out no longer.

'Which is it to-day,' I asked, 'morphine or cocaine?'

He raised his eyes languidly from the old black-letter volume which he had opened.

'It is cocaine,' he said, 'a seven-per-cent. solution. Would you care to try it?'

'No, indeed,' I answered brusquely. 'My constitution has not got over the Afghan campaign yet. I cannot afford to throw any extra strain upon it.'

He smiled at my vehemence. 'Perhaps you are right, Watson,' he said. 'I suppose that its influence is physically a bad one. I find it, however, so transcendently stimulating and clarifying to the mind that its secondary action is a matter of small moment.'

'But consider!' I said earnestly. 'Count the cost! Your brain may, as you say, be

roused and excited, but it is a pathological
and morbid process, which involves increased
tissue-change and may at least leave a perma-
nent weakness.   You know, too, what a
black reaction comes upon you.   Surely the
game is hardly worth the candle.   Why
should you, for a mere passing pleasure, risk
the loss of those great powers with which
you have been endowed?   Remember that I
speak not only as one comrade to another,
but as a medical man to one for whose constitution he is to some extent answerable.'

He did not seem offended.   On the contrary, he put his finger-tips together, and
leaned his elbows on the arms of his chair,
like one who has a relish for conversation.

'My mind,' he said, 'rebels at stagnation.
Give me problems, give me work, give me
the most abstruse cryptogram, or the most in-
tricate analysis, and I am in my own proper
atmosphere.   I can dispense then with

artificial stimulants. But I abhor the dull routine of existence. I crave for mental exaltation. That is why I have chosen my own particular profession, or rather created it, for I am the only one in the world.'

'The only unofficial detective?' I said, raising my eyebrows.

'The only unofficial consulting detective,' he answered. 'I am the last and highest court of appeal in detection. When Gregson, or Lestrade, or Athelney Jones are out of their depths—which, by the way, is their normal state—the matter is laid before me. I examine the data, as an expert, and pronounce a specialist's opinion. I claim no credit in such cases. My name figures in no newspaper. The work itself, the pleasure of finding a field for my peculiar powers, is my highest reward. But you have yourself had some experience of my methods of work in the Jefferson Hope case.'

'Yes, indeed,' said I cordially. 'I was never so struck by anything in my life. I even embodied it in a small brochure, with the somewhat fantastic title of "A Study in Scarlet."'

He shook his head sadly.

'I glanced over it,' said he. 'Honestly, I cannot congratulate you upon it. Detection is, or ought to be, an exact science, and should be treated in the same cold and unemotional manner. You have attempted to tinge it with romanticism, which produces much the same effect as if you worked a love-story or an elopement into the fifth proposition of Euclid.'

'But the romance was there,' I remonstrated. 'I could not tamper with the facts.'

'Some facts should be suppressed, or, at least, a just sense of proportion should be observed in treating them. The only point in the case which deserved mention was the curious analytical reasoning from effects to causes, by which I succeeded in unravelling it.'

I was annoyed at this criticism of a work which had been specially designed to please him. I confess, too, that I was irritated by the egotism which seemed to demand that every line of my pamphlet should be devoted to his own special doings. More than once during the years that I had lived with him in Baker Street I had observed that a small vanity underlay my companion's quiet and didactic manner. I made no remark, however, but sat nursing my wounded leg. I had had a Jezail bullet through it some time before, and, though it did not prevent me from walking, it ached wearily at every change of the weather.

' My practice has extended recently to the Continent,' said Holmes, after awhile, filling up his old briar-root pipe. ' I was consulted last week by François le Villard, who, as you probably know, has come rather to the front lately in the French detective service. He has all the Celtic power of quick intuition, but he is deficient in the wide range of exact knowledge which is essential to the higher developments of his art. The case was concerned with a will, and possessed some features of interest. I was able to refer him to two parallel cases, the one at Riga in 1857, and the other at St. Louis in 1871, which have suggested to him the true solution. Here is the letter which I had this morning acknowledging my assistance.'

He tossed over, as he spoke, a crumpled sheet of foreign notepaper. I glanced my eyes down it, catching a profusion of notes of admiration, with stray 'magnifiques,' 'ccup-de-maltres,' and 'tours-de-force,' all testifying to the ardent admiration of the Frenchman.

'He speaks as a pupil to his master,' said I.

'Oh, he rates my assistance too highly,' said Sherlock Holmes lightly. 'He has considerable gifts himself. He possesses two out of the three qualities necessary for the ideal detective. He has the power of observation and that of deduction. He is only wanting in knowledge, and that may come in time. He is now translating my small works into French.'

'Your works?'

'Oh, didn't you know?' he cried, laughing. 'Yes, I have been guilty of several monographs. They are all upon technical subjects. Here, for example, is one "Upon the Distinction between the Ashes of the Various Tobaccos." In it I enumerate a hundred and forty forms of cigar, cigarette, and pipe tobacco, with coloured plates illustrating the difference in the ash. It is a point which is

continually turning up in criminal trials, and
which is sometimes of supreme importance as
a clue. If you can say definitely, for example,
that some murder had been done by a man
who was smoking an Indian lunkah, it
obviously narrows your field of search. To
the trained eye there is as much difference
between the black ash of a Trichinopoly and
the white fluff of bird's-eye as there is between
a cabbage and a potato.'

'You have an extraordinary genius for
minutiæ,' I remarked.

'I appreciate their importance. Here is
my monograph upon the tracing of footsteps,
with some remarks upon the uses of plaster
of Paris as a preserver of impresses. Here,
too, is a curious little work upon the influence of a trade upon the form of the hand,
with lithotypes of the hands of slaters, sailors,
cork-cutters, compositors, weavers, and
diamond-polishers. That is a matter of great

practical interest to the scientific detective—
especially in cases of unclaimed bodies, or in
discovering the antecedents of criminals. But
I weary you with my hobby.'

'Not at all,' I answered earnestly. 'It is
of the greatest interest to me, especially since
I have had the opportunity of observing your
practical application of it. But you spoke
just now of observation and deduction.
Surely the one to some extent implies the
other.'

'Why, hardly,' he answered, leaning back
luxuriously in his armchair, and sending up
thick blue wreaths from his pipe. 'For
example, observation shows me that you have
been to the Wigmore Street Post-Office this
morning, but deduction lets me know that
when there you despatched a telegram.'

'Right!' said I. 'Right on both points!
But I confess that I don't see how you
arrived at it. It was a sudden impulse upon

my part, and I have mentioned it to no
one.'

'It is simplicity itself,' he remarked,
chuckling at my surprise — 'so absurdly
simple that an explanation is superfluous ;
and yet it may serve to define the limits of
observation and of deduction.   Observation
tells me that you have a little reddish mould
adhering to your instep.   Just opposite the
Wigmore Street Office they have taken up
the pavement and thrown up some earth,
which lies in such a way that it is difficult to
avoid treading in it in entering.   The earth is
of this peculiar reddish tint which is found, as
far as I know, nowhere else in the neighbourhood.   So much is observation.   The rest is
deduction.'

'How, then, did you deduce the telegram ?'

'Why, of course I knew that you had not
written a letter, since I sat opposite to you

all morning. I see also in your open desk
there that you have a sheet of stamps and a
thick bundle of postcards. What could you
go into the post-office for, then, but to send a
wire? Eliminate all other factors, and the
one which remains must be the truth.'

' In this case it certainly is so,' I replied,
after a little thought. 'The thing, however,
is, as you say, of the simplest. Would you
think me impertinent if I were to put your
theories to a more severe test?'

' On the contrary,' he answered ; 'it would
prevent me from taking a second dose of
cocaine. I should be delighted to look into
any problem which you might submit to me.'

' I have heard you say that it is difficult for
a man to have any object in daily use without
leaving the impress of his individuality upon
it in such a way that a trained observer might
read it. Now, I have here a watch which has
recently come into my possession. Would you

have the kindness to let me have an opinion upon the character or habits of the late owner?'

I handed him over the watch with some slight feeling of amusement in my heart, for the test was, as I thought, an impossible one, and I intended it as a lesson against the somewhat dogmatic tone which he occasionally assumed. He balanced the watch in his hand, gazed hard at the dial, opened the back, and examined the works, first with his naked eyes and then with a powerful convex lens. I could hardly keep from smiling at his crestfallen face when he finally snapped the case to and handed it back.

'There are hardly any data,' he remarked. 'The watch has been recently cleaned, which robs me of my most suggestive facts.'

'You are right,' I answered. 'It was cleaned before being sent to me.'

In my heart I accused my companion of putting forward a most lame and impotent excuse to cover his failure. What data could he expect from an uncleaned watch ?

'Though unsatisfactory, my research has not been entirely barren,' he observed, staring up at the ceiling with dreamy, lack-lustre eyes. 'Subject to your correction, I should judge that the watch belonged to your elder brother, who inherited it from your father.'

'That you gather, no doubt, from the H. W. upon the back ?'

'Quite so. The W. suggests your own name. The date of the watch is nearly fifty years back, and the initials are as old as the watch: so it was made for the last genera-tion. Jewellery usually descends to the eldest son, and he is most likely to have the same name as the father. Your father has, if I remember right, been dead many years. It has, therefore, been in the hands of your eldest brother.'

'Right, so far,' said I. 'Anything else?'

'He was a man of untidy habits—very untidy and careless. He was left with good prospects, but he threw away his chances, lived for some time in poverty with occasional short intervals of prosperity, and finally, taking to drink, he died. That is all I can gather.'

I sprang from my chair and limped impatiently about the room with considerable bitterness in my heart.

'This is unworthy of you, Holmes,' I said. 'I could not have believed that you would have descended to this. You have made inquiries into the history of my unhappy brother, and you now pretend to deduce this knowledge in some fanciful way. You cannot expect me to believe that you have read all this from his old watch! It is unkind, and, to speak plainly, has a touch of charlatanism in it'

'My dear doctor,' said he kindly, 'pray accept my apologies. Viewing the matter as an abstract problem, I had forgotten how personal and painful a thing it might be to you. I assure you, however, that I never even knew that you had a brother until you handed me the watch.'

'Then how in the name of all that is wonderful did you get these facts? They are absolutely correct in every particular.'

'Ah, that is good luck. I could only say what was the balance of probability. I did not at all expect to be so accurate.'

'But it was not mere guess-work?'

'No, no: I never guess. It is a shocking habit — destructive to the logical faculty. What seems strange to you is only so because you do not follow my train of thought or observe the small facts upon which large inferences may depend. For example, I began by stating that your

2

brother was careless. When you observe
the lower part of that watch-case you notice
that it is not only dinted in two places, but
it is cut and marked all over from the habit
of keeping other hard objects, such as coins
or keys, in the same pocket. Surely it is no
great feat to assume that a man who treats
a fifty-guinea watch so cavalierly must be a
careless man. Neither is it a very far-
fetched inference that a man who inherits
one article of such value is pretty well provided for in other respects.'

I nodded, to show that I followed his
reasoning.

'It is very customary for pawnbrokers in
England, when they take a watch, to scratch
the number of the ticket with a pin-point
upon the inside of the case. It is more
handy than a label, as there is no risk of
the number being lost or transposed. There
are no less than four such numbers visible

to my lens on the inside of this case. Inference—that your brother was often at low
water. Secondary inference—that he had
occasional bursts of prosperity, or he could
not have redeemed the pledge. Finally, I
ask you to look at the inner plate, which
contains the keyhole. Look at the thousands of scratches all round the hole—marks
where the key has slipped. What sober
man's key could have scored those grooves ?
But you will never see a drunkard's watch
without them. He winds it at night, and
he leaves these traces of his unsteady hand.
Where is the mystery in all this ?'

'It is as clear as daylight,' I answered.
' I regret the injustice which I did you. I
should have had more faith in your marvellous
faculty. May I ask whether you have any
professional inquiry on foot at present ?'

'None. Hence the cocaine. I cannot
live without brain-work. What else is there

to live for? Stand at the window here.
Was ever such a dreary, dismal, unprofitable
world? See how the yellow fog swirls
down the street and drifts across the dun-
coloured houses. What could be more
hopelessly prosaic and material? What is
the use of having powers, doctor, when one
has no field upon which to exert them?
Crime is commonplace, existence is commonplace, and no qualities save those which are
commonplace have any function upon earth.'

I had opened my mouth to reply to this
tirade, when, with a crisp knock, our landlady entered, bearing a card upon the brass
salver.

'A young lady for you, sir,' she said,
addressing my companion.

'Miss Mary Morstan,' he read. 'Hum! I
have no recollection of the name. Ask the
young lady to step up, Mrs. Hudson. Don't
go, doctor. I should prefer that you remain.'

CHAPTER II.

MISS MORSTAN entered the room with a firm step and an outward composure of manner. She was a blonde young lady, small, dainty, well gloved, and dressed in the most perfect taste. There was, however, a plainness and simplicity about her costume which bore with it a suggestion of limited means. The dress was a sombre grayish beige, untrimmed and unbraided, and she wore a small turban of the same dull hue, relieved only by a suspicion of white feather in the side. Her face had neither regularity of feature nor beauty of complexion, but her expression was sweet and amiable, and her large blue eyes were singularly spiritual and sympathetic. In an experience of women which extends over many nations and three separate continents, I have never looked upon a face which gave a clearer promise of a refined and sensitive nature. I could not but observe that as she took the seat which Sherlock Holmes placed for her, her lip trembled, her hand quivered, and she showed every sign of intense inward agitation.

'I have come to you, Mr. Holmes,' she said, 'because you once enabled my employer, Mrs. Cecil Forrester, to unravel a little domestic complication. She was much impressed by your kindness and skill.'

'Mrs. Cecil Forrester,' he repeated thoughtfully. 'I believe that I was of some slight service to her. The case, however, as I remember it, was a very simple one.'

'She did not think so. But at least you cannot say the same of mine. I can hardly

imagine anything more strange, more utterly
inexplicable, than the situation in which I
find myself.'

Holmes rubbed his hands, and his eyes
glistened. He leaned forward in his chair
with an expression of extraordinary concen-
tration upon his clear-cut, hawk-like features.

' State your case,' said he, in brisk, business
tones.

I felt that my position was an embarrassing
one.

'You will, I am sure, excuse me,' I said,
rising from my chair.

To my surprise, the young lady held up
her gloved hand to detain me.

' If your friend,' she said, 'would be good
enough to stop, he might be of inestimable
service to me.'

I relapsed into my chair.

' Briefly,' she continued, 'the facts are these.
My father was an officer in an Indian regi-

ment, who sent me home when I was quite
a child.   My mother was dead, and I had no
relative in England.   I was placed, however,
in a comfortable boarding establishment at
Edinburgh, and there I remained until I was
seventeen years of age.   In the year 1878
my father, who was senior captain of his
regiment, obtained twelve months' leave and
came home.   He telegraphed to me from
London that he had arrived all safe, and
directed me to come down at once, giving
the Langham Hotel as his address.   His
message, as I remember, was full of kindness
and love.   On reaching London I drove to
the Langham, and was informed that Captain
Morstan was staying there, but that he had
gone out the night before and had not
returned.   I waited all day without news of
him.   That night, on the advice of the
manager of the hotel, I communicated with
the police, and next morning we advertised

in all the papers. Our inquiries led to no result; and from that day to this no word has ever been heard of my unfortunate father. He came home with his heart full of hope, to find some peace, some comfort, and instead——'

She put her hand to her throat, and a choking sob cut short the sentence.

' The date ?' asked Holmes, opening his note-book.

' He disappeared upon the 3rd of December, 1878—nearly ten years ago.'

' His luggage ?'

' Remained at the hotel. There was nothing in it to suggest a clue—some clothes, some books, and a considerable number of curiosities from the Andaman Islands. He had been one of the officers in charge of the convict-guard there.'

' Had he any friends in town ?'

'Only one that we know of — Major

Sholto, of his own regiment, the 34th Bombay
Infantry.   The Major had retired some little
time before, and lived at Upper Norwood.
We communicated with him, of course, but
he did not even know that his brother officer
was in England.'

' A singular case,' remarked Holmes.

' I have not yet described to you the most
singular part.   About six years ago—to be
exact, upon the 4th of May, 1882—an advertisement appeared in the *Times* asking
for the address of Miss Mary Morstan, and
stating that it would be to her advantage to
come forward.   There was no name or address appended.   I had at that time just
entered the family of Mrs. Cecil Forrester
in the capacity of governess.   By her advice
I published my address in the advertisement
column.   The same day there arrived
through the post a small cardboard box
addressed to me, which I found to contain a

very large and lustrous pearl. No word of writing was enclosed. Since then every year upon the same date there has always appeared a similar box, containing a similar pearl, without any clue as to the sender. They have been pronounced by an expert to be of a rare variety and of considerable value. You can see for yourselves that they are very handsome.'

She opened a flat box as she spoke, and showed me six of the finest pearls that I had ever seen.

'Your statement is most interesting,' said Sherlock Holmes. 'Has anything else occurred to you?'

'Yes, and no later than to-day. That is why I have come to you. This morning I received this letter, which you will perhaps read for yourself.'

'Thank you,' said Holmes. 'The envelope too, please. Post-mark, London, S.W.

Date, July 7. Hum! Man's thumb-mark on corner—probably postman. Best quality paper. Envelopes at sixpence a packet. Particular man in his stationery. No address. " Be at the third pillar from the left outside the Lyceum Theatre to-night at seven o'clock. If you are distrustful bring two friends. You are a wronged woman, and shall have justice. Do not bring police. If you do, all will be in vain. Your unknown friend." Well, really, this is a very pretty little mystery! What do you intend to do, Miss Morstan ?'

' That is exactly what I want to ask you.'

' Then we shall most certainly go—you and I and—yes, why Dr. Watson is the very man. Your correspondent says two friends. He and I have worked together before.'

' But would he come ?' she asked, with something appealing in her voice and expression.

'I shall be proud and happy,' said I, fervently, 'if I can be of any service.'

'You are both very kind,' she answered. 'I have led a retired life, and have no friends whom I could appeal to. If I am here at six it will do, I suppose?'

'You must not be later,' said Holmes. 'There is one other point, however. Is this handwriting the same as that upon the pearl-box addresses?'

'I have them here,' she answered, producing half a dozen pieces of paper.

'You are certainly a model client. You have the correct intuition. Let us see, now.' He spread out the papers upon the table, and gave little darting glances from one to the other. 'They are disguised hands, except the letter,' he said presently; 'but there can be no question as to the authorship. See how the irrepressible Greek *e* will break out, and see the twirl of the final *s*. They are

undoubtedly by the same person. I should
not like to suggest false hopes, Miss Morstan,
but is there any resemblance between this
hand and that of your father ?'

'Nothing could be more unlike.'

'I expected to hear you say so. We shall
look out for you, then, at six. Pray allow me
to keep the papers. I may look into the
matter before then. It is only half-past three.
Au revoir, then.'

'*Au revoir*,' said our visitor; and with a
bright, kindly glance from one to the other of
us, she replaced her pearl-box in her bosom
and hurried away.

Standing at the window, I watched her
walking briskly down the street, until the
gray turban and white feather were but a
speck in the sombre crowd.

'What a very attractive woman !' I exclaimed, turning to my companion.

He had lit his pipe again, and was leaning

back with drooping eyelids. ' Is she ?' he said languidly ; ' I did not observe.'

' You really are an automaton—a calculating machine,' I cried. ' There is something positively inhuman in you at times.'

He smiled gently.

' It is of the first importance,' he said, ' not to allow your judgment to be biased by personal qualities. A client is to me a mere unit, a factor in a problem. The emotional qualities are antagonistic to clear reasoning. I assure you that the most winning woman I ever knew was hanged for poisoning three little children for their insurance-money, and the most repellant man of my acquaintance is a philanthropist who has spent nearly a quarter of a million upon the London poor.'

' In this case, however——'

' I never make exceptions. An exception disproves the rule. Have you ever had occasion to study character in handwriting ?

What do you make of this fellow's scribble ?'

'It is legible and regular,' I answered. 'A man of business habits and some force of character.'

Holmes shook his head.

'Look at his long letters,' he said. 'They hardly rise above the common herd. That *d* might be an *a*, and that *l* an *e*. Men of character always differentiate their long letters, however illegibly they may write. There is vacillation in his *k*'s and self-esteem in his capitals. I am going out now. I have some few references to make. Let me recommend this book—one of the most remarkable ever penned. It is Winwood Reade's " Martyrdom of Man." I shall be back in an hour.'

I sat in the window with the volume in my hand, but my thoughts were far from the daring speculations of the writer. My mind ran upon our late visitor—her smiles, the deep rich tones of her voice, the strange mystery which overhung her life. If she were seventeen at the time of her father's disappearance she must be seven-and-twenty now—a sweet age, when youth has lost its self-consciousness and become a little sobered by experience. So I sat and mused, until such dangerous thoughts came into my head that I hurried away to my desk and plunged furiously into the latest treatise upon pathology. What was I, an army surgeon with a weak leg and a weaker banking account, that I should dare to think of such things? She was a unit, a factor—nothing more. If my future were black, it was better surely to face it like a man than to attempt to brighten it by mere will-o'-the-wisps of the imagination.

CHAPTER III.

IN QUEST OF A SOLUTION.

IT was half-past five before Holmes returned. He was bright, eager, and in excellent spirits, a mood which in his case alternated with fits of the blackest depression.

'There is no great mystery in this matter,' he said, taking the cup of tea which I had poured out for him; 'the facts appear to admit of only one explanation.'

'What! you have solved it already?'

'Well, that would be too much to say. I have discovered a suggestive fact, that is all. It is, however, *very* suggestive. The details are still to be added. I have just found, on consulting the back files of the *Times*, that

Major Sholto, of Upper Norwood, late of the 34th Bombay Infantry, died upon the 28th of April, 1882.'

' I may be very obtuse, Holmes, but I fail to see what this suggests.'

'No? You surprise me. Look at it in this way, then. Captain Morstan disappears. The only person in London whom he could have visited is Major Sholto. Major Sholto denies having heard that he was in London. Four years later Sholto dies. *Within a week of his death* Captain Morstan's daughter receives a valuable present, which is repeated from year to year, and now culminates in a letter which describes her as a wronged woman. What wrong can it refer to except this deprivation of her father ? And why should the presents begin immediately after Sholto's death, unless it is that Sholto's heir knows something of the mystery and desires to make compensation ? Have you any

alternative theory which will meet **the**
facts ?'

'But what a strange compensation! And
how strangely made! Why, too, should he
write a letter now, rather than six years ago?
Again, the letter speaks of giving her justice.
What justice can she have? It is too much
to suppose that her father is still alive.
There is no other injustice in her case that
you know of.'

'There are difficulties; there are certainly
difficulties,' said Sherlock Holmes pensively;
'but our expedition of to-night will solve them
all. Ah, here is a four-wheeler, and Miss Morstan is inside. Are you all ready? Then we had
better go down, for it is a little past the hour.'

I picked up my hat and my heaviest stick,
but I observed that Holmes took his revolver
from his drawer and slipped it into his
pocket. It was clear that he thought that
our night's work might be a serious one.

Miss Morstan was muffled in a dark cloak, and her sensitive face was composed, but pale. She must have been more than woman if she did not feel some uneasiness at the strange enterprise upon which we were em-barking, yet her self-control was perfect, and she readily answered the few additional questions which Sherlock Holmes put to her.

' Major Sholto was a very particular friend of papa's,' she said. ' His letters were full of allusions to the Major. He and papa were in command of the troops at the Andaman Islands, so they were thrown a great deal together. By the way, a curious paper was found in papa's desk which no one could understand. I don't suppose that it is of the slightest importance, but I thought you might care to see it, so I brought it with me. It is here.'

Holmes unfolded the paper carefully and

smoothed it out upon his knee. He then very methodically examined it all over with his double lens.

'It is paper of native Indian manufacture,' he remarked. 'It has at some time been pinned to a board. The diagram upon it appears to be a plan of part of a large building with numerous halls, corridors, and passages. At one point is a small cross done in red ink, and above it is "3.37 from left," in faded pencil-writing. In the left-hand corner is a curious hieroglyphic like four crosses in a line with their arms touching. Beside it is written, in very rough and coarse characters, "The sign of the four—Jonathan Small, Mahomet Singh, Abdullah Khan, Dost Akbar." No, I confess that I do not see how this bears upon the matter. Yet it is evidently a document of importance. It has been kept carefully in a pocket-book; for the one side is as clean as the other.'

'It was in his pocket-book that we found it.'

'Preserve it carefully, then, Miss Morstan, for it may prove to be of use to us. I begin to suspect that this matter may turn out to be much deeper and more subtle than I at first supposed. I must reconsider my ideas.'

He leaned back in the cab, and I could see by his drawn brow and his vacant eye that he was thinking intently. Miss Morstan and I chatted in an undertone about our present expedition and its possible outcome, but our companion maintained his impenetrable reserve until the end of our journey.

It was a September evening, and not yet seven o'clock, but the day had been a dreary one, and a dense drizzly fog lay low upon the great city. Mud-coloured clouds drooped sadly over the muddy streets. Down the Strand the lamps were but misty splotches of

diffused light which threw a feeble circular
glimmer upon the slimy pavement. The
yellow glare from the shop-windows streamed
out into the steamy, vaporous air, and threw
a murky, shifting radiance across the crowded
thoroughfare. There was, to my mind,
something eerie and ghost-like in the endless
procession of faces which flitted across these
narrow bars of light—sad faces and glad,
haggard and merry. Like all human kind,
they flitted from the gloom into the light,
and so back into the gloom once more. I
am not subject to impressions, but the dull,
heavy evening, with the strange business
upon which we were engaged, combined to
make me nervous and depressed. I could
see from Miss Morstan's manner that she
was suffering from the same feeling. Holmes
alone could rise superior to petty influences.
He held his open notebook upon his knee,
and from time to time he jotted down figures

and memoranda in the light of his pocket-lantern.

At the Lyceum Theatre the crowds were already thick at the side-entrances. In front a continuous stream of hansoms and four-wheelers were rattling up, discharging their cargoes of shirt-fronted men and be-shawled, be-diamonded women. We had hardly reached the third pillar, which was our rendezvous, before a small, dark, brisk man in the dress of a coachman accosted us.

'Are you the parties who come with Miss Morstan?' he asked.

'I am Miss Morstan, and these two gentlemen are my friends,' said she.

He bent a pair of wonderfully penetrating and questioning eyes upon us.

'You will excuse me, miss,' he said, with a certain dogged manner, 'but I was to ask you to give me your word that neither of your companions is a police-officer.'

'I give you my word on that,' she answered.

He gave a shrill whistle, on which a street arab led across a four-wheeler and opened the door. The man who had addressed us mounted to the box, while we took our places inside. We had hardly done so before the driver whipped up his horse, and we plunged away at a furious pace through the foggy streets.

The situation was a curious one. We were driving to an unknown place, on an unknown errand. Yet our invitation was either a com- plete hoax — which was an inconceivable hypothesis—or else we had good reason to think that important issues might hang upon our journey. Miss Morstan's demeanour was as resolute and collected as ever. I en- deavoured to cheer and amuse her by reminiscences of my adventures in Afghani- stan ; but, to tell the truth, I was myself so excited at our situation, and so curious as to our destination, that my stories were slightly involved. To this day she declares that I told her one moving anecdote as to how a musket looked into my tent at the dead of night, and how I fired a double-barrelled tiger cub at it. At first I had some idea as to the direction in which we were driving ; but soon, what with our pace, the fog, and my own limited knowledge of London, I lost my bearings, and knew nothing, save that we seemed to be going a very long way. Sherlock Holmes was never at fault, however, and he muttered the names as the cab rattled through squares and in and out by tortuous by-streets.

' Rochester Row,' said he. ' Now Vincent Square. Now we come out on the Vauxhall Bridge Road. We are making for the Surrey side, apparently. Yes, I thought so. Now we are on the bridge. You can catch glimpses of the river.

We did indeed get a fleeting view of a
stretch of the Thames, with the lamps shining
upon the broad, silent water; but our cab
dashed on, and was soon involved in a
labyrinth of streets upon the other side.

'Wordsworth Road,' said my companion.
'Priory Road. Lark Hall Lane. Stockwell
Place. Robert Street. Cold Harbour Lane.
Our quest does not appear to take us to very
fashionable regions.'

We had indeed reached a questionable
and forbidding neighbourhood. Long lines
of dull brick houses were only relieved by
the coarse glare and tawdry brilliancy of
public-houses at the corner. Then came
rows of two-storied villas, each with a front-
ing of miniature garden, and then again
interminable lines of new, staring brick
buildings—the monster tentacles which the
giant city was throwing out into the country.
At last the cab drew up at the third house in

a new terrace. None of the other houses were inhabited, and that at which we stopped was as dark as its neighbours, save for a single glimmer in the kitchen-window. On our knocking, however, the door was instantly thrown open by a Hindoo servant, clad in a yellow turban, white loose-fitting clothes, and a yellow sash. There was something strangely incongruous in this Oriental figure framed in the commonplace doorway of a third-rate suburban dwelling-house.

'The Sahib awaits you,' said he, and even as he spoke there came a high, piping voice from some inner room.

'Show them in to me, khitmutgar,' it cried. 'Show them straight in to me.'

CHAPTER IV.

THE STORY OF THE BALD-HEADED MAN.

WE followed the Indian down a sordid and common passage, ill-lit and worse furnished, until he came to a door upon the right, which he threw open. A blaze of yellow light streamed out upon us, and in the centre of the glare there stood a small man with a very high head, a bristle of red hair all round the fringe of it, and a bald, shining scalp which shot out from among it like a mountain-peak from fir-trees. He writhed his hands together as he stood, and his features were in a perpetual jerk—now smiling, now scowling, but never for an instant in repose. Nature had given him a pendulous lip, and a too

visible line of yellow and irregular teeth,
which he strove feebly to conceal by con-
stantly passing his hand over the lower part
of his face. In spite of his obtrusive bald-
ness, he gave the impression of youth. In
point of fact, he had just turned his thirtieth
year.

'Your servant, Miss Morstan,' he kept
repeating, in a thin, high voice. 'Your
servant, gentlemen. Pray step into my little
sanctum. A small place, miss, but furnished
to my own liking. An oasis of art in the
howling desert of South London.'

We were all astonished by the appearance
of the apartment into which he invited us.
In that sorry house it looked as out of place
as a diamond of the first water in a setting of
brass. The richest and glossiest of curtains
and tapestries draped the walls, looped back
here and there to expose some richly-mounted
painting or Oriental vase. The carpet was

of amber and black, so soft and so thick that
the foot sank pleasantly into it, as into a bed
of moss.   Two great tiger-skins thrown
athwart it increased the suggestion of Eastern
luxury, as did a huge hookah which stood
upon a mat in the corner.   A lamp in the
fashion of a silver dove was hung from an
almost invisible golden wire in the centre of
the room.   As it burned it filled the air
with a subtle and aromatic odour.

'Mr. Thaddeus Sholto,' said the little man,
still jerking and smiling.   'That is my name.
You are Miss Morstan, of course.   And these
gentlemen——'

'This is Mr. Sherlock Holmes, and this
Dr. Watson.'

'A doctor, eh?' cried he, much excited.
'Have you your stethoscope?   Might I ask
you—would you have the kindness?   I have
grave doubts as to my mitral valve, if you
would be so very good.   The aortic I may

rely upon, but I should value your opinion upon the mitral.

I listened to his heart, as requested, but was unable to find anything amiss, save, indeed, that he was in an ecstasy of fear, for he shivered from head to foot.

' It appears to be normal,' I said. ' You have no cause for uneasiness.'

' You will excuse my anxiety, Miss Morstan,' he remarked airily. ' I am a great sufferer, and I have long had suspicions as to that valve. I am delighted to hear that they are unwarranted. Had your father, Miss Morstan, refrained from throwing a strain upon his heart, he might have been alive now.'

I could have struck the man across the face, so hot was I at this callous and off-hand reference to so delicate a matter. Miss Morstan sat down, and her face grew white to the lips.

4

'I knew in my heart that he was dead,' said she.

'I can give you every information,' said he; 'and, what is more, I can do you justice; and I will, too, whatever Brother Bartholomew may say. I am so glad to have your friends here, not only as an escort to you, but also as witnesses to what I am about to do and say. The three of us can show a bold front to Brother Bartholomew. But let us have no outsiders—no police or officials. We can settle everything satisfactorily among ourselves, without any interference. Nothing would annoy Brother Bartholomew more than any publicity.'

He sat down upon a low settee, and blinked at us inquiringly with his weak, watery blue eyes.

'For my part,' said Holmes, 'whatever you may choose to say will go no further.'

I nodded to show my agreement.

'That is well! That is well!' said he. 'May I offer you a glass of Chianti, Miss Morstan? Or of Tokay? I keep no other wines. Shall I open a flask? No? Well, then, I trust that you have no objection to tobacco-smoke, to the balsamic odour of the Eastern tobacco. I am a little nervous, and I find my hookah an invaluable sedative.'

He applied a taper to the great bowl, and the smoke bubbled merrily through the rose-water. We sat all three in a semicircle, with our heads advanced and our chins upon our hands, while the strange, jerky little fellow, with his high, shining head, puffed uneasily in the centre.

'When I first determined to make this communication to you,' said he, 'I might have given you my address; but I feared that you might disregard my request and bring unpleasant people with you. I took the liberty, therefore, of making an appoint

4—2

ment in such a way that my man Williams might be able to see you first. I have complete confidence in his discretion, and he had orders, if he were dissatisfied, to proceed no further in the matter. You will excuse these precautions, but I am a man of somewhat retiring, and I might even say refined tastes, and there is nothing more unæsthetic than a policeman. I have a natural shrinking from all forms of rough materialism. I seldom come in contact with the rough crowd. I live, as you see, with some little atmosphere of elegance around me. I may call myself a patron of the arts. It is my weakness. The landscape is a genuine Corot, and, though a connoisseur might perhaps throw a doubt upon that Salvator Rosa, there cannot be the least question about the Bouguereau. I am partial to the modern French school.'

'You will excuse me, Mr. Sholto,' said Miss Morstan, 'but I am here at your

request to learn something which you desire
to tell me. It is very late, and I should
desire the interview to be as short as
possible.'

'At the best it must take some time, he
answered ; 'for we shall certainly have to go
to Norwood and see Brother Bartholomew.
We shall all go and try if we can get the
better of Brother Bartholomew. He is very
angry with me for taking the course which
has seemed right to me. I had quite high
words with him last night. You cannot
imagine what a terrible fellow he is when he
is angry.'

'If we are to go to Norwood, it would
perhaps be as well to start at once,' I ventured
to remark.

He laughed until his ears were quite red.

'That would hardly do,' he cried. 'I don't
know what he would say if I brought you in
that sudden way. No, I must prepare you

by showing you how we all stand to each
other.   In the first place, I must tell you
that there are several points in the story of
which I am myself ignorant.   I can only lay
the facts before you as far as I know them
myself.

'My father was, as you may have guessed,
Major John Sholto, once of the Indian army.
He retired some eleven years ago, and came
to live at Pondicherry Lodge in Upper
Norwood.   He had prospered in India, and
brought back with him a considerable sum
of money, a large collection of valuable
curiosities, and a staff of native servants.
With these advantages he bought himself a
house, and lived in great luxury.   My twin-
brother Bartholomew and I were the only
children.

'I very well remember the sensation which
was caused by the disappearance of Captain
Morstan.   We read the details in the papers,

and, knowing that he had been a friend of our father's, we discussed the case freely in his presence. He used to join in our speculations as to what could have happened. Never for an instant did we suspect that he had the whole secret hidden in his own breast, that of all men he alone knew the fate of Arthur Morstan.

'We did know, however that some mystery, some positive danger, overhung our father. He was very fearful of going out alone, and he always employed two prize-fighters to act as porters at Pondicherry Lodge. Williams, who drove you to-night, was one of them. He was once light-weight champion of England. Our father would never tell us what it was he feared, but he had a most marked aversion to men with wooden legs. On one occasion he actually fired his revolver at a wooden-legged man, who proved to be a harmless tradesman canvassing for orders.

We had to pay a large sum to hush the matter up. My brother and I used to think this a mere whim of my father's; but events have since led us to change our opinion.

' Early in 1882 my father received a letter from India which was a great shock to him. He nearly fainted at the breakfast-table when he opened it, and from that day he sickened to his death. What was in the letter we could never discover, but I could see as he held it that it was short and written in a scrawling hand. He had suffered for years from an enlarged spleen, but he now became rapidly worse, and towards the end of April we were informed that he was beyond all hope, and that he w shed to make a last communication to us.

' When we entered his room he was propped up with pillows and breathing heavily. He besought us to lock the door and to come upon either side of the bed. Then, grasping our hands, he made a remarkable statement to us, in a voice which was broken as much by emotion as by pain. I shall try and give it to you in his own very words.

' " I have only one thing," he said, " which weighs upon my mind at this supreme moment. It is my treatment of poor Morstan's orphan. The cursed greed which has been my besetting sin through life has withheld from her the treasure, half at least of which should have been hers. And yet I have made no use of it myself, so blind and foolish a thing is avarice. The mere feeling of possession has been so dear to me that I could not bear to share it with another. See that chaplet tipped with pearls beside the quinine-bottle. Even that I could not bear to part with, although I had got it out with the design of sending it to her. You, my sons, will give her a fair share of the Agra treasure. But send her nothing—not even

the chaplet—until I am gone.   After all,
men have been as bad as this and have
recovered.

'" I will tell you how Morstan died," he
continued.   " He had suffered for years from
a weak heart, but he concealed it from every
one.   I alone knew it.   When in India, he
and I, through a remarkable chain of circumstances, came into possession of a considerable
treasure.   I brought it over to England, and
on the night of Morstan's arrival he came
straight over here to claim his share.   He
walked over from the station, and was
admitted by my faithful old Lal Chowdar,
who is now dead.   Morstan and I had a
difference of opinion as to the division of the
treasure, and we came to heated words.
Morstan had sprung out of his chair in a
paroxysm of anger, when he suddenly pressed
his hand to his side, his face turned a dusky
hue, and he fell backwards, cutting his head

against the corner of the treasure-chest. When I stooped over him I found, to my horror, that he was dead.

' " For a long time I sat half distracted, wondering what I should do. My first impulse was, of course, to call for assistance ; but I could not but recognise that there was every chance that I would be accused of his murder. His death at the moment of a quarrel, and the gash in his head, would be black against me. Again, an official inquiry could not be made without bringing out some facts about the treasure, which I was particularly anxious to keep secret. He had told me that no soul upon earth knew where he had gone. There seemed to be no necessity why any soul ever should know.

' " I was still pondering over the matter, when, looking up, I saw my servant, Lal Chowdar, in the doorway. He stole in and bolted the door behind him. ' Do not fear,

Sahib,' he said ; ' no one need know that you have killed him. Let us hide him away, and who is the wiser ?' ' I did not kill him,' said I. Lal Chowdar shook his head and smiled ' I heard it all, Sahib,' said he ; ' I heard you quarrel, and I heard the blow. But my lips are sealed. All are asleep in the house. Let us put him away together.' That was enough to decide me. If my own servant could not believe my innocence, how could I hope to make it good before twelve foolish tradesmen in a jury-box ? Lal Chowdar and I disposed of the body that night, and within a few days the London papers were full of the mysterious disappearance of Captain Morstan. You will see from what I say that I can hardly be blamed in the matter. My fault lies in the fact that we concealed not only the body, but also the treasure, and that I have clung to Morstan's share as well as to my own. I wish you, therefore, to make restitution. Put

your ears down to my mouth. The treasure
is hidden in——"

'At this instant a horrible change came
over his expression ; his eyes stared wildly,
his jaw dropped, and he yelled, in a voice
which I can never forget, " Keep him out !
For Christ's sake keep him out !" We both
stared round at the window behind us upon
which his gaze was fixed. A face was looking
in at us out of the darkness. We could see
the whitening of the nose where it was
pressed against the glass. It was a bearded,
hairy face, with wild cruel eyes and an
expression of concentrated malevolence. My
brother and I rushed towards the window, but
the man was gone. When we returned to
my father his head had dropped and his pulse
had ceased to beat.

'We searched the garden that night, but
found no sign of the intruder, save that just
under the window a single footmark was

visible in the flower-bed. But for that one
trace, we might have thought that our imagi-
nations had conjured up that wild, fierce face.
We soon, however, had another and a more
striking proof that there were secret agencies
at work all round us. The window of my
father's room was found open in the morning,
his cupboards and boxes had been rifled, and
upon his chest was fixed a torn piece of paper,
with the words " The sign of the four "
scrawled across it. What the phrase meant,
or who our secret visitor may have been, we
never knew. As far as we can judge, none of
my father's property had been actually stolen,
though everything had been turned out. My
brother and I naturally associated this peculiar
incident with the fear which haunted my
father during his life ; but it is still a complete
mystery to us.'

The little man stopped to relight his
hookah and puffed thoughtfully for a few

moments. We had all sat absorbed, listening
to his extraordinary narrative. At the short
account of her father's death Miss Morstan
had turned deadly white, and for a moment I
feared that she was about to faint. She
rallied, however, on drinking a glass of water
which I quietly poured our for her from a
Venetian carafe upon the side-table. Sherlock
Holmes leaned back in his chair with an
abstracted expression and the lids drawn low
over his glittering eyes. As I glanced at
him I could not but think how on that very
day he had complained bitterly of the com-
monplaceness of life. Here at least was a
problem which would tax his sagacity to the
utmost. Mr. Thaddeus Sholto looked from
one to the other of us with an obvious pride
at the effect which his story had produced,
and then continued between the puffs of his
overgrown pipe.

' My brother and I,' said he, ' were, as you

may imagine, much excited as to the treasure which my father had spoken of. For weeks and for months we dug and delved in every part of the garden without discovering its whereabouts. It was maddening to think that the hiding-place was on his very lips at the moment that he died. We could judge the splendour of the missing riches by the chaplet which he had taken out. Over this chaplet my brother Bartholomew and I had some little discussion. The pearls were evidently of great value, and he was averse to part with them, for, between friends, my brother was himself a little inclined to my father's fault. He thought, too, that if we parted with the chaplet it might give rise to gossip, and finally bring us into trouble. It was all that I could do to persuade him to let me find out Miss Morstan's address and send her a detached pearl at fixed intervals, so that at least she might never feel destitute.'

'It was a kindly thought,' said our companion earnestly; 'it was extremely good of you.'

The little man waved his hand deprecatingly.

'We were your trustees,' he said; 'that was the view which I took of it, though brother Bartholomew could not altogether see it in that light. We had plenty of money ourselves. I desired no more. Besides, it would have been such bad taste to have treated a young lady in so scurvy a fashion. "Le mauvais goût mène au crime." The French have a very neat way of putting these things. Our difference of opinion on this subject went so far that I thought it best to set up rooms for myself; so I left Pondicherry Lodge, taking the old khitmutgar and Williams with me. Yesterday, however, I learn that an event of extreme importance has occurred. The treasure has been discovered. I instantly

5

communicated with Miss Morstan, and it only remains for us to drive out to Norwood and demand our share. I explained my views last night to brother Bartholomew, so we shall be expected, if not welcome, visitors.'

Mr. Thaddeus Sholto ceased, and sat twitching on his luxurious settee. We all remained silent, with our thoughts upon the new development which the mysterious business had taken. Holmes was the first to spring to his feet.

'You have done well, sir, from first to last,' said he. 'It is possible that we may be able to make you some small return by throwing some light upon that which is still dark to you. But, as Miss Morstan remarked just now, it is late, and we had best put the matter through without delay.'

Our new acquaintance very deliberately coiled up the tube of his hookah, and produced from behind a curtain a very long

befrogged topcoat with Astrakhan collar and
cuffs. This he buttoned tightly up, in spite
of the extreme closeness of the night, and
finished his attire by putting on a rabbit-
skin cap with hanging lappets which covered
the ears, so that no part of him was visible
save his mobile and peaky face.

'My health is somewhat fragile,' he remarked, as he led the way down the passage.
'I am compelled to be a valetudinarian.'

Our cab was awaiting us outside, and our
programme was evidently prearranged, for
the driver started off at once at a rapid pace.
Thaddeus Sholto talked incessantly, in a
voice which rose high above the rattle of
the wheels.

'Bartholomew is a clever fellow,' said he.
'How do you think he found out where the
treasure was? He had come to the conclusion that it was somewhere indoors: so
he worked out all the cubic space of the

5—2

house, and made measurements everywhere, so that not one inch should be unaccounted for. Among other things, he found that the height of the building was seventy-four feet, but on adding together the heights of all the separate rooms, and making every allowance for the space between, which he ascertained by borings, he could not bring the total to more than seventy feet. There were four feet unaccounted for. These could only be at the top of the building. He knocked a hole, therefore, in the lath and plaster ceiling of the highest room, and there, sure enough, he came upon another little garret above it, which had been sealed up and was known to no one. In the centre stood the treasure-chest, resting upon two rafters. He lowered it through the hole, and there it lies. He computes the value of the jewels at not less than half a million sterling.'

At the mention of this gigantic sum we all stared at one another open-eyed. Miss Morstan, could we secure her rights, would change from a needy governess to the richest heiress in England. Surely it was the place of a loyal friend to rejoice at such news; yet I am ashamed to say that selfishness took me by the soul, and that my heart turned as heavy as lead within me. I stammered out some few halting words of congratulation, and then sat downcast, with my head drooped, deaf to the babble of our new acquaintance. He was clearly a confirmed hypochondriac, and I was dreamily conscious that he was pouring forth interminable trains of symptoms, and imploring information as to the composition and action of innumerable quack nostrums, some of which he bore about in a leather case in his pocket. I trust that he may not remember any of the answers which I gave him that night.

Holmes declares that he overheard me caution him against the great danger of taking more than two drops of castor-oil, while I recommended strychnine in large doses as a sedative. However that may be, I was certainly relieved when our cab pulled up with a jerk and the coachman sprang down to open the door.

'This, Miss Morstan, is Pondicherry Lodge,' said Mr. Thaddeus Sholto, as he handed her out.

CHAPTER V.

THE TRAGEDY OF PONDICHERRY LODGE.

It was nearly eleven o'clock when we reached this final stage of our night's adventures. We had left the damp fog of the great city behind us, and the night was fairly fine. A warm wind blew from the westward, and heavy clouds moved slowly across the sky, with half a moon peeping occasionally through the rifts. It was clear-enough to see for some distance, but Thaddeus Sholto took down one of the side-lamps from the carriage to give us a better light upon our way.

Pondicherry Lodge stood in its own grounds, and was girt round with a very high

stone wall topped with broken glass.   A
single narrow iron-clamped door formed the
only means of entrance.   On this our guide
knocked with a peculiar postman-like rat-tat.

'Who is there ?' cried a gruff voice from
within.

' It is I, McMurdo.   You surely know my
knock by this time.'

There was a grumbling sound and a
clanking and jarring of keys.   The door
swung heavily back, and a short, deep-
chested man stood in the opening, with the
yellow light of the lantern shining upon
his protruded face and twinkling, distrustful
eyes.

' That you, Mr. Thaddeus ?   But who are
the others ?   I had no orders about them
from the master.'

'No, McMurdo ?   You surprise me!   I
told my brother last night that I should bring
some friends.'

'He hain't been out o' his room to-day, Mr. Thaddeus, and I have no orders. You know very well that I must stick to regulations. I can let you in, but your friends they must just stop where they are.'

This was an unexpected obstacle. Thaddeus Sholto looked about him in a perplexed and helpless manner.

'This is too bad of you, McMurdo!' he said. 'If I guarantee them, that is enough for you. There is the young lady, too. She cannot wait on the public road at this hour.'

'Very sorry, Mr. Thaddeus,' said the porter inexorably. 'Folk may be friends o' yours, and yet no friends o' the master's. He pays me well to do my duty, and my duty I'll do. I don't know none o' your friends.'

'Oh yes, you do, McMurdo,' cried Sherlock Holmes genially. 'I don't think you can have forgotten me. Don't you remember the amateur who fought three rounds with you at Alison's rooms on the night of your benefit four years back ?'

'Not Mr. Sherlock Holmes!' roared the prize-fighter. 'God's truth! how could I have mistook you? If instead o' standin' there so quiet you had just stepped up and given me that cross-hit of yours under the jaw, I'd ha' known you without a question. Ah, you're one that has wasted your gifts, you have! You might have aimed high, if you had joined the fancy.'

'You see, Watson, if all else fails me, I have still one of the scientific professions open to me,' said Holmes, laughing. 'Our friend won't keep us out in the cold now, I am sure.'

'In you come, sir, in you come—you and your friends,' he answered. 'Very sorry, Mr. Thaddeus, but orders are very strict. Had to be certain of your friends before I let them in.'

Inside, a gravel path wound through desolate grounds to a huge clump of a house,
square and prosaic, all plunged in shadow
save where a moonbeam struck one corner
and glimmered in a garret window. The
vast size of the building, with its gloom and
its deathly silence, struck a chill to the heart.
Even Thaddeus Sholto seemed ill at ease,
and the lantern quivered and rattled in his
hand.

'I cannot understand it,' he said. 'There
must be some mistake. I distinctly told
Bartholomew that we should be here, and yet
there is no light in his window. I do not
know what to make of it.'

'Does he always guard the premises in
this way?' asked Holmes.

'Yes; he has followed my father's custom.
He was the favourite son, you know, and I
sometimes think that my father may have
told him more than he ever told me. That

is Bartholomew's window up there where
the moonshine strikes.   It is quite bright,
but there is no light from within, I
think.'

'None,' said Holmes.   'But I see the
glint of a light in that little window beside
the door.'

'Ah, that is the housekeeper's room.   That
is where old Mrs. Bernstone sits.   She can
tell us all about it.   But perhaps you would
not mind waiting here for a minute or two,
for if we all go in together, and she has had
no word of our coming, she may be alarmed.
But, hush ! what is that ?'

He held up the lantern, and his hand shook
until the circles of light flickered and wavered
all round us.   Miss Morstan seized my wrist,
and we all stood, with thumping hearts,
straining our ears.   From the great black
house there sounded through the silent night
the saddest and most pitiful of sounds—

the shrill, broken whimpering of a frightened
woman.

'It is Mrs. Bernstone,' said Sholto. 'She
is the only woman in the house. Wait here.
I shall be back in a moment.'

He hurried for the door, and knocked in
his peculiar way. We could see a tall old
woman admit him, and sway with pleasure at
the very sight of him.

'Oh, Mr. Thaddeus, sir, I am so glad you
have come! I am so glad you have come,
Mr. Thaddeus, sir!'

We heard her reiterated rejoicings until
the door was closed and her voice died away
into a muffled monotone.

Our guide had left us the lantern. Holmes
swung it slowly round, and peered keenly at
the house, and at the great rubbish-heaps
which cumbered the grounds. Miss Morstan
and I stood together, and her hand was in
mine. A wondrous subtle thing is love, for

here were we two, who had never seen each other before that day, between whom no word or even look of affection had ever passed, and yet now in an hour of trouble our hands instinctively sought for each other. I have marvelled at it since, but at the time it seemed the most natural thing that I should go out to her so, and, as she has often told me, there was in her also the instinct to turn to me for comfort and protection. So we stood hand-in-hand, like two children, and there was peace in our hearts for all the dark things that surrounded us.

'What a strange place!' she said, looking round.

'It looks as though all the moles in England had been let loose in it. I have seen something of the sort on the side of a hill near Ballarat, where the prospectors had been at work.'

'And from the same cause,' said Holmes.

' These are the traces of the treasure-seekers.
You must remember that they were six years
looking for it. No wonder that the grounds
look like a gravel-pit.'

At that moment the door of the house
burst open, and Thaddeus Sholto came
running out, with his hands thrown forward
and terror in his eyes.

' There is something amiss with Bartholomew!' he cried. ' I am frightened! My
nerves cannot stand it.'

He was, indeed, half blubbering with fear,
and his twitching, feeble face peeping out
from the great Astrakhan collar had the
helpless, appealing expression of a terrified
child.

' Come into the house,' said Holmes, in his
crisp, firm way.

' Yes, do !' pleaded Thaddeus Sholto. ' I
really do not feel equal to giving directions.'

We all followed him into the housekeeper's

room, which stood upon the left-hand side of
the passage.   The old woman was pacing up
and down with a scared look and restless,
picking fingers, but the sight of Miss
Morstan appeared to have a soothing effect
upon her.

'God bless your sweet, calm face!' she
cried, with an hysterical sob.   'It does me
good to see you. Oh, but I have been sorely
tried this day!'

Our companion patted her thin, work-worn
hand, and murmured some few words of
kindly, womanly comfort which brought the
colour back into the other's bloodless cheeks.

'Master has locked himself in, and will
not answer me,' she explained.   'All day I
have waited to hear from him, for he often
likes to be alone; but an hour ago I feared
that something was amiss, so I went up and
peeped through the keyhole. You must go
up, Mr. Thaddeus—you must go up and look

for yourself. I have seen Mr. Bartholomew Sholto in joy and in sorrow for ten long years, but I never saw him with such a face on him as that.'

Sherlock Holmes took the lamp and led the way, for Thaddeus Sholto's teeth were chattering in his head. So shaken was he that I had to pass my hand under his arm as we went up the stairs, for his knees were trembling under him. Twice as we ascended Holmes whipped his lens out of his pocket and carefully examined marks which appeared to me to be mere shapeless smudges of dust upon the cocoanut-matting which served as a stair-carpet. He walked slowly from step to step, holding the lamp low, and shooting keen glances to right and left. Miss Morstan had remained behind with the frightened housekeeper.

The third flight of stairs ended in a straight passage of some length, with a great picture

6

in Indian tapestry upon the right of it and
three doors upon the left.   Holmes advanced
along it in the same slow and methodical way,
while we kept close at his heels, with our long
black shadows streaming backwards down the
corridor.   The third door was that which we
were seeking.   Holmes knocked without
receiving any answer, and then tried to turn
the handle and force it open.   It was locked
on the inside, however, and by a broad and
powerful bolt, as we could see when we set
our lamp up against it.   The key being
turned, however, the hole was not entirely
closed.   Sherlock Holmes bent down to it,
and instantly rose again with a sharp intaking
of the breath.

 'There is something devilish in this,
Watson,' said he, more moved than I had
ever before seen him.   'What do you make
of it ?'

 I stooped to the hole, and recoiled in

horror. Moonlight was streaming into the room, and it was bright with a vague and shifty radiance. Looking straight at me, and suspended, as it were, in the air, for all beneath was in shadow, there hung a face— the very face of our companion Thaddeus. There was the same high, shining head, the same circular bristle of red hair, the same bloodless countenance. The features were set, however, in a horrible smile, a fixed and unnatural grin, which in that still and moonlit room was more jarring to the nerves than any scowl or contortion. So like was the face to that of our little friend that I looked round at him to make sure that he was indeed with us. Then I recalled to mind that he had mentioned to us that his brother and he were twins.

'This is terrible!' I said to Holmes 'What is to be done ?'

'The door must come down,' he answered,

6—2

and, springing against it, he put all his weight upon the lock.

It creaked and groaned, but did not yield. Together we flung ourselves upon it once more, and this time it gave way with a sudden snap, and we found ourselves within Bartholomew Sholto's chamber.

It appeared to have been fitted up as a chemical laboratory. A double line of glass-stoppered bottles was drawn up upon the wall opposite the door, and the table was littered over with Bunsen burners, test-tubes, and retorts. In the corners stood carboys of acid in wicker baskets. One of these appeared to leak or to have been broken, for a stream of dark-coloured liquid had trickled out from it, and the air was heavy with a peculiarly pungent, tar-like odour. A set of steps stood at one side of the room, in the midst of a litter of lath and plaster, and above them there was an opening in the ceiling large enough for a man to pass through. At the foot of the steps a long coil of rope was thrown carelessly together.

By the table, in a wooden arm-chair, the master of the house was seated all in a heap, with his head sunk upon his left shoulder, and that ghastly, inscrutable smile upon his face. He was stiff and cold, and had clearly been dead many hours. It seemed to me that not only his features, but all his limbs, were twisted and turned in the most fantastic fashion. By his hand upon the table there lay a peculiar instrument—a brown, close-grained stick, with a stone head like a hammer, rudely lashed on with coarse twine. Beside it was a torn sheet of note-paper with some words scrawled upon it. Holmes glanced at it, and then handed it to me.

'You see,' he said, with a significant raising of the eyebrows.

In the light of the lantern I read, with a thrill of horror, ' The sign of the four.'

' In God's name, what does it all mean ?' I asked.

' It means murder,' said he, stooping over the dead man. 'Ah ! I expected it. Look here !'

He pointed to what looked like a long dark thorn stuck in the skin just above the ear.

' It looks like a thorn,' said I.

' It is a thorn. You may pick it out. But be careful, for it is poisoned.'

I took it up between my finger and thumb. It came away from the skin so readily that hardly any mark was left behind. One tiny speck of blood showed where the puncture had been.

' This is all an insoluble mystery to me,' said I. ' It grows darker instead of clearer.'

' On the contrary,' he answered, ' it clears

every instant. I only require a few missing links to have an entirely connected case.'

We had almost forgotten our companion's presence since we entered the chamber. He was still standing in the doorway, the very picture of terror, wringing his hands and moaning to himself. Suddenly, however, he broke out into a sharp, querulous cry.

'The treasure is gone!' he said. 'They have robbed him of the treasure! There is the hole through which we lowered it. I helped him to do it! I was the last person who saw him! I left him here last night, and I heard him lock the door as I came down-stairs.'

'What time was that?'

'It was ten o'clock. And now he is dead, and the police will be called in, and I shall be suspected of having had a hand in it. Oh yes, I am sure I shall. But you don't think so, gentlemen? Surely you don't think that it was I ?   Is it likely that I would have brought you here if it were I ?   Oh dear! oh dear !   I know that I shall go mad !'

He jerked his arms and stamped his feet in a kind of convulsive frenzy.

'You have no reason for fear, Mr. Sholto,' said Holmes kindly, putting his hand upon his shoulder ; 'take my advice, and drive down to the station to report the matter to the police.   Offer to assist them in every way. We shall wait here until your return.'

The little man obeyed in a half-stupefied fashion, and we heard him stumbling down the stairs in the dark.

CHAPTER VI.

SHERLOCK HOLMES GIVES A DEMONSTRATION.

'Now, Watson,' said Holmes, rubbing his hands, 'we have half an hour to ourselves. Let us make good use of it. My case is, as I have told you, almost complete; but we must not err on the side of over-confidence. Simple as the case seems now, there may be something deeper underlying it.'

'Simple!' I ejaculated.

'Surely,' said he, with something of the air of a clinical professor expounding to his class. 'Just sit in the corner there, that your foot-prints may not complicate matters. Now to work! In the first place, how did these folk

come, and how did they go ? The door has
not been opened since last night. How of
the window ?' He carried the lamp across to
it, muttering his observations aloud the while
but addressing them to himself rather than to
me. Window is snibbed on the inner side.
Framework is solid. No hinges at the side.
Let us open it. No water-pipe near. Roof
quite out of reach. Yet a man has mounted
by the window. It rained a little last night.
Here is the print of a foot in mould upon the
sill. And here is a circular muddy mark, and
here again upon the floor, and here again by
the table. See here, Watson! This is really
a very pretty demonstration.'

I looked at the round, well-defined muddy
discs.

' That is not a footmark,' said I.

' It is something much more valuable to us.
It is the impression of a wooden stump. You
see here on the sill is the boot-mark, a heavy

boot with a broad metal heel, and beside it is the mark of the timber-toe.'

'It is the wooden-legged man.'

'Quite so. But there has been someone else—a very able and efficient ally. Could you scale that wall, doctor?'

I looked out of the open window. The moon still shone brightly on that angle of the house. We were a good sixty feet from the ground, and, look where I would, I could see no foothold, nor as much as a crevice in the brickwork.

'It is absolutely impossible,' I answered.

'Without aid it is so. But suppose you had a friend up here who lowered you this good stout rope which I see in the corner, securing one end of it to this great hook in the wall. Then, I think, if you were an active man, you might swarm up, wooden leg and all. You would depart, of course, in the same fashion, and your ally would draw up the rope, untie it from the hook, shut the window, snib it on the inside, and get away in the way that he originally came. As a minor point, it may be noted,' he continued, fingering the rope, ' that our wooden-legged friend, though a fair climber, was not a professional sailor. His hands were far from horny. My lens discloses more than one blood-mark, especially towards the end of the rope, from which I gather that he slipped down with such velocity that he took the skin off his hand.'

' This is all very well,' said I ; ' but the thing becomes more unintelligible than ever. How about this mysterious ally ? How came he into the room ?'

' Yes, the ally !' repeated Holmes pensively. ' There are features of interest about this ally. He lifts the case from the regions of the commonplace. I fancy that this ally breaks fresh ground in the annals of crime in this

country—though parallel cases suggest themselves from India, and, if my memory serves
me, from Senegambia.'

' How came he, then ?' I reiterated. ' The
door is locked ; the window is inaccessible.
Was it through the chimney ?'

' The grate is much too small,' he answered.
' I had already considered that possibility.'

' How, then ?' I persisted.

' You will not apply my precept,' he said,
shaking his head. ' How often have I said to
you that when you have eliminated the impossible, whatever remains, *however impro-
bable*, must be the truth ? We know that he
did not come through the door, the window,
or the chimney. We also know that he could
not have been concealed in the room, as there
is no concealment possible. Whence, then,
did he come ?'

' He came through the hole in the roof!' I
cried.

'Of course he did. He must have done so.
If you will have the kindness to hold the lamp
for me, we shall now extend our researches to
the room above—the secret room in which the
treasure was found.'

He mounted the steps, and, seizing a rafter
with either hand, he swung himself up into
the garret. Then, lying on his face, he
reached down for the lamp, and held it while
I followed him.

The chamber in which we found ourselves
was about ten feet one way and six the other.
The floor was formed by the rafters, with thin
lath-and-plaster between, so that in walking
one had to step from beam to beam. The
roof ran up to an apex, and was evidently the
inner shell of the true roof of the house.
There was no furniture of any sort, and the
accumulated dust of years lay thick upon the
floor.

'Here you are, you see,' said Sherlock

Holmes, putting his hand against the sloping wall. ' This is a trapdoor which leads out on to the roof. I can press it back, and here is the roof itself, sloping at a gentle angle. This, then, is the way by which Number One entered. Let us see if we can find some other traces of his individuality ?'

He held down the lamp to the floor, and as he did so I saw for the second time that night a startled, surprised look come over his face. For myself, as I followed his gaze, my skin was cold under my clothes. The floor was covered thickly with the prints of a naked foot—clear, well-defined, perfectly formed, but scarce half the size of those of an ordinary man.'

' Holmes,' I said, in a whisper, 'a child has done this horrid thing.'

He had recovered his self-possession in an instant.

' I was staggered for the moment,' he said,

'but the thing is quite natural. My memory failed me, or I should have been able to foretell it. There is nothing more to be learned here. Let us go down.'

'What is your theory, then, as to those footmarks?' I asked eagerly, when we had regained the lower room once more.

'My dear Watson, try a little analysis yourself,' said he, with a touch of impatience. 'You know my methods. Apply them, and it will be instructive to compare results.'

'I cannot conceive anything which will cover the facts,' I answered.

'It will be clear enough to you soon,' he said, in an off-hand way. 'I think that there is nothing else of importance here, but I will look.'

He whipped out his lens and a tape measure, and hurried about the room on his knees, measuring, comparing, examining, with his long thin nose only a few inches from the planks, and his beady eyes gleaming and deep-set like those of a bird. So swift, silent, and furtive were his movements, like those of a trained bloodhound picking out a scent, that I could not but think what a terrible criminal he would have made had he turned his energy and sagacity against the law, instead of exerting them in its defence. As he hunted about, he kept muttering to himself, and finally he broke out into a loud crow of delight.

'We are certainly in luck,' said he. 'We ought to have very little trouble now. Number One has had the misfortune to tread in the creosote. You can see the outline of the edge of his small foot here at the side of this evil-smelling mess. The carboy has been cracked, you see, and the stuff has leaked out.'

'What then ?' I asked.

'Why, we have got him, that's all,' said

7

he. 'I know a dog that would follow that scent to the world's end. If a pack can track a trailed herring across a shire, how far can a specially-trained hound follow so pungent a smell as this ? It sounds like a sum in tne rule of three. The answer should give us the—— But hallo ! here are the accredited representatives of the law.'

Heavy steps and the clamour of loud voices were audible from below, and the hall door shut with a loud crash.

'Before they come,' said Holmes, 'just put your hand here on this poor fellow's arm, and here on his leg. What do you feel ?'

'The muscles are as hard as a board,' I answered.

'Quite so. They are in a state of extreme contraction, far exceeding the usual *rigor mortis.* Coupled with this distortion of the face, this Hippocratic smile, or "*risus sardonicus,*" as the old writers called it, what conclusion would it suggest to your mind ?'

'Death from some powerful vegetable alkaloid,' I answered, 'some strychnine-like substance which would produce tetanus.'

'That was the idea which occurred to me the instant I saw the drawn muscles of the face. On getting into the room I at once looked for the means by which the poison had entered the system. As you saw, I discovered a thorn which had been driven or shot with no great force into the scalp. You observe that the part struck was that which would be turned towards the hole in the ceiling if the man were erect in his chair. Now examine this thorn.'

I took it up gingerly and held it in the light of the lantern. It was long, sharp, and black, with a glazed look near the point as though some gummy substance had dried

upon it. The blunt end had been trimmed
and rounded off with a knife.

'Is that an English thorn ?' he asked.

'No, it certainly is not.'

'With all these data you should be able
to draw some just inference. But here are
the regulars : so the auxiliary forces may
beat a retreat.'

As he spoke, the steps which had been
coming nearer sounded loudly on the
passage, and a very stout, portly man in a
gray suit strode heavily into the room. He
was red-faced, burly, and plethoric, with a
pair of very small twinkling eyes which
looked keenly out from between swollen and
puffy pouches. He was closely followed by
an inspector in uniform, and by the still
palpitating Thaddeus Sholto.

'Here's a business !' he cried, in a
muffled, husky voice. 'Here's a pretty
business ! But who are all these ? Why,

the house seems to be as full as a rabbit-warren !'

'I think you must recollect me, Mr. Athelney Jones,' said Holmes quietly.

' Why, of course I do !' he wheezed. ' It's Mr. Sherlock Holmes, the theorist. Remember you ! I'll never forget how you lectured us all on causes and inferences and effects in the Bishopgate jewel case. It's true you set us on the right track ; but you'll own now that it was more by good luck than good guidance.'

' It was a piece of very simple reasoning.'

' Oh, come, now, come ! Never be ashamed to own up. But what is all this ? Bad business ! Bad business ! Stern facts here—no room for theories. How lucky that I happened to be out at Norwood over another case ! I was at the station when the message arrived. What d'you think the man died of ?'

'Oh, this is hardly a case for me to theorize over,' said Holmes dryly.

'No, no. Still, we can't deny that you hit the nail on the head sometimes. Dear me! Door locked, I understand. Jewels worth half a million missing. How was the window?'

'Fastened; but there are steps on the sill.'

'Well, well, if it was fastened the steps could have nothing to do with the matter. That's common-sense. Man might have died in a fit; but then the jewels are missing. Ha! I have a theory. These flashes come upon me at times. — Just step outside, sergeant, and you, Mr. Sholto. Your friend can remain.—What do you think of this, Holmes? Sholto was, on his own confession, with his brother last night. The brother died in a fit, on which Sholto walked off with the treasure? How's that?'

'On which the dead man very considerately got up and locked the door on the inside.'

'Hum! There's a flaw there. Let us apply commonsense to the matter. This Thaddeus Sholto *was* with his brother; there *was* a quarrel : so much we know. The brother is dead and the jewels are gone. So much also we know. No one saw the brother from the time Thaddeus left him. His bed had not been slept in. Thaddeus is evidently in a most disturbed state of mind. His appearance is—well, not attractive. You see that I am weaving my web round Thaddeus. The net begins to close upon him.'

'You are not quite in possession of the facts yet,' said Holmes. 'This splinter of wood, which I have every reason to believe to be poisoned, was in the man's scalp where you still see the mark; this card, inscribed as you see it, was on the table, and beside

it lay this rather curious stone-headed instrument. How does all that fit into your
theory ?'

'Confirms it in every respect,' said the fat
detective, pompously. 'House is full of
Indian curiosities. Thaddeus brought this
up, and if this splinter be poisonous, Thaddeus
may as well have made murderous use of it as
any other man. The card is some hocus-
pocus—a blind, as like as not. The only
question is, how did he depart ? Ah, of
course, here is a hole in the roof.'

With great activity, considering his bulk,
he sprang up the steps and squeezed through
into the garret, and immediately afterwards
we heard his exulting voice proclaiming that
he had found the trap-door.'

'He can find something,' remarked Holmes,
shrugging his shoulders ; 'he has occasional
glimmerings of reason. *Il n'y a pas des sots
si incommodes que ceux qui ont de l'esprit !*

'You see!' said Athelney Jones, reappearing down the steps again ; ' facts are better than theories, after all. My view of the case is confirmed. There is a trap-door communicating with the roof, and it is partly open.'

' It was I who opened it.'

' Oh, indeed ! You did notice it, then ?' He seemed a little crestfallen at the discovery. ' Well, whoever noticed it, it shows how our gentleman got away. Inspector !'

' Yes, sir,' from the passage.

' Ask Mr. Sholto to step this way.— Mr. Sholto, it is my duty to inform you that anything which you may say will be used against you. I arrest you in the Queen's name as being concerned in the death of your brother.

' There, now ! Didn't I tell you !' cried the poor little man, throwing out his hands, and looking from one to the other of us.

' Don't trouble yourself about it, Mr. Sholto,' said Holmes ; ' I think that I can engage to clear you of the charge.'

' Don't promise too much, Mr. Theorist, don't promise too much !' snapped the detective.   ' You may find it a harder matter than you think.'

' Not only will I clear him, Mr. Jones, but I will make you a free present of the name and description of one of the two people who were in this room last night.   His name, I have every reason to believe, is Jonathan Small.   He is a poorly-educated man, small, active, with his right leg off, and wearing a wooden stump which is worn away upon the inner side.   His left boot has a coarse, square-toed sole, with an iron band round the heel.   He is a middle-aged man, much sun-burned, and has been a convict.   These few indications may be of some assistance to you, coupled with the fact that there is a good deal of skin missing from the palm of his hand. The other man——'

'Ah! the other man?' asked Athelney Jones in a sneering voice, but impressed none the less, as I could easily see, by the precision of the other's manner.

' Is a rather curious person,' said Sherlock Holmes, turning upon his heel. 'I hope before very long to be able to introduce you to the pair of them. A word with you, Watson.'

He led me out to the head of the stair.

'This unexpected occurrence,' he said, 'has caused us rather to lose sight of the original purpose of our journey.'

'I have just been thinking so,' I answered; 'it is not right that Miss Morstan should remain in this stricken house.'

'No. You must escort her home. She lives with Mrs. Cecil Forrester, in Lower Camberwell, so it is not very far. I will wait

for you here if you will drive out again.   Or
perhaps you are too tired ?'

'By no means.   I don't think I could rest
until I know more of this fantastic business.
I have seen something of the rough side of
life, but I give you my word that this quick
succession of strange surprises to-night has
shaken my nerve completely.   I should like,
however, to see the matter through with you,
now that I have got so far.'

'Your presence will be of great service to
me,' he answered.   'We shall work the case
out independently, and leave this fellow Jones
to exult over any mare's-nest which he may
choose to construct.   When you have dropped
Miss Morstan, I wish you to go on to No. 3,
Pinchin Lane, down near the water's edge at
Lambeth.   The third house on the right
hand side is a bird-stuffer's ; Sherman is the
name.   You will see a weasel holding a young
rabbit in the window.   Knock old Sherman

up, and tell him, with my compliments, that I
want Toby at once. You will bring Toby
back in the cab with you.'

A dog, I suppose.'

'Yes, a queer mongrel, with a most
amazing power of scent. I would rather
have Toby's help than that of the whole
detective force of London.'

'I shall bring him then,' said I. 'It is one
now. I ought to be back before three, if I
can get a fresh horse.'

'And I,' said Holmes, 'shall see what I
can learn from Mrs. Bernstone, and from the
Indian servant, who, Mr. Thaddeus tells me,
sleeps in the next garret. Then I shall study
the great Jones's methods and listen to his not
too delicate sarcasms. " *Wir sind gewohnt
dass die Menschen verhöhnen was sie nicht
verstehen.*" Goethe is always pithy.'

CHAPTER VII.

THE EPISODE OF THE BARREL.

THE police had brought a cab with them, and in this I escorted Miss Morstan back to her home. After the angelic fashion of women, she had borne trouble with a calm face as long as there was someone weaker than herself to support, and I had found her bright and placid by the side of the frightened housekeeper. In the cab, however, she first turned faint, and then burst into a passion of weeping—so sorely had she been tried by the adventures of the night. She has told me since that she thought me cold and distant upon that journey. She little guessed the struggle within my breast, or the effort of self-restraint which held me back. My sympathies and my love went out to her, even as my hand had in the garden. I felt that years of the conventionalities of life could not teach me to know her sweet, brave nature as had this one day of strange experiences. Yet there were two thoughts which sealed the words of affection upon my lips. She was weak and helpless, shaken in mind and nerve. It was to take her at a disadvantage to obtrude love upon her at such a time. Worse still, she was rich. If Holmes's researches were successful, she would be an heiress. Was it fair, was it honourable, that a half-pay surgeon should take such advantage of an intimacy which chance had brought about? Might she not look upon me as a mere vulgar fortune-seeker? I could not bear to risk that such a thought should cross her mind. This Agra treasure intervened like an impassable barrier between us.

It was nearly two o'clock when we reached
Mrs. Cecil Forester's. The servants had
retired hours ago, but Mrs. Forrester had
been so interested by the strange message
which Miss Morstan had received that she
had sat up in the hope of her return. She
opened the door herself, a middle-aged,
graceful woman, and it gave me joy to see
how tenderly her arm stole round the other's
waist, and how motherly was the voice in
which she greeted her. She was clearly no
mere paid dependant, but an honoured friend.
I was introduced, and Mrs. Forrester earnestly
begged me to step in and to tell her our
adventures. I explained, however, the importance of my errand, and promised faith-
fully to call and report any progress which we
might make with the case. As we drove
away I stole a glance back, and I still seem
to see that little group on the step—the two
graceful, clinging figures, the half-opened

door, the hall-light shining through stained glass, the barometer, and the bright stair-rods. It was soothing to catch even that passing glimpse of a tranquil English home in the midst of the wild, dark business which had absorbed us.

And the more I thought of what had happened, the wilder and darker it grew. I reviewed the whole extraordinary sequence of events as I rattled on through the silent, gaslit streets. There was the original problem : that at least was pretty clear now. The death of Captain Morstan, the sending of the pearls, the advertisement, the letter—we had had light upon all those events. They had only led us, however, to a deeper and far more tragic mystery. The Indian treasure, the curious plan found among Morstan's baggage, the strange scene at Major Sholto's death, the rediscovery of the treasure immediately followed by the murder of the dis-

8

coverer, the very singular accompaniments
to the crime, the footsteps, the remarkable
weapons, the words upon the card, corre-
sponding with those upon Captain Morstan's
chart—here was indeed a labyrinth in which
a man less singularly endowed than my fellow-
lodger might well despair of ever finding the
clue.

Pinchin Lane was a row of shabby, two-
storied brick houses in the lower quarter of
Lambeth. I had to knock for some time
at No. 3 before I could make any impression.
At last, however, there was the glint of a
candle behind the blind, and a face looked out
at the upper window.

'Go on, you drunken vagabone,' said the
face. 'If you kick up any more row, I'll
open the kennels and let out forty-three dogs
upon you.'

'If you'll let one out, it's just what I have
come for,' said I.

'Go on!' yelled the voice. 'So help me gracious, I have a wiper in this bag, an I'll drop it on your 'ead if you don't hook it!'

'But I want a dog,' I cried.

'I won't be argued with!' shouted Mr. Sherman. 'Now stand clear; for when I say "three," down goes the wiper.'

'Mr. Sherlock Holmes——' I began; but the words had a most magical effect, for the window instantly slammed down, and within a minute the door was unbarred and open. Mr. Sherman was a lanky, lean old man, with stooping shoulders, a stringy neck, and blue-tinted glasses.

'A friend of Mr. Sherlock is always welcome,' said he. 'Step in, sir. Keep clear of the badger, for he bites. Ah, naughty, naughty! would you take a nip at the gentleman?' This to a stoat which thrust its wicked head and red eyes between the bars

8 – 2

of its cage. ' Don't mind that, sir ; it's only
a slowworm.   It hain't got no fangs, so I
gives it the run o' the room, for it keeps the
beetles down.   You must not mind my bein'
just a little short wi' you at first, for I'm
guyed at by the children, and there's many a
one just comes down this lane to knock me
up.   What was it that Mr. Sherlock Holmes
wanted, sir ?'

' He wanted a dog of yours.'

' Ah ! that would be Toby.'

' Yes, Toby was the name.'

' Toby lives at No. 7 on the left here.

He moved slowly forward with his candle
among the queer animal family which he had
gathered round him.   In the uncertain,
shadowy light I could see dimly that there
were glancing, glimmering eyes peeping down
at us from every cranny and corner.   Even
the rafters above our heads were lined by
solemn fowls, who lazily shifted their weight

from one leg to the other as our voices disturbed their slumbers.

Toby proved to be an ugly, long-haired,
lop-eared creature, half spaniel and half
lurcher, brown and white in colour, with a
very clumsy, waddling gait. It accepted,
after some hesitation, a lump of sugar which
the old naturalist handed to me, and, having
thus sealed an alliance, it followed me to the
cab, and made no difficulties about accom-
panying me. It had just struck three on the
Palace clock when I found myself back once
more at Pondicherry Lodge. The ex-prize-
fighter McMurdo had, I found, been arrested
as an accessory, and both he and Mr. Sholto
had been marched off to the station. Two
constables guarded the narrow gate, but they
allowed me to pass with the dog on my men-
tioning the detective's name.

Holmes was standing on the doorstep, with
his hands in his pockets, smoking his pipe.

'Ah, you have him there!' said he. 'Good dog, then! Athelney Jones has gone. We have had an immense display of energy since you left. He has arrested not only friend Thaddeus, but the gatekeeper, the house-keeper, and the Indian servant. We have the place to ourselves, but for a sergeant upstairs. Leave the dog here, and come up.'

We tied Toby to the hall table, and re-ascended the stairs. The room was as we had left it, save that a sheet had been draped over the central figure. A weary-looking police-sergeant reclined in the corner.

'Lend me your bull's-eye, sergeant,' said my companion. 'Now tie this bit of card round my neck, so as to hang it in front of me. Thank you. Now I must kick off my boots and stockings. Just you carry them down with you, Watson. I am going to do a little climbing. And dip my handkerchief

into the creosote. That will do. Now come
up into the garret with me for a moment.'

We clambered up through the hole.
Holmes turned his light once more upon the
footsteps in the dust.

'I wish you particularly to notice these
footmarks,' he said. 'Do you observe anything noteworthy about them ?'

'They belong,' I said, 'to a child or a small
woman.'

'Apart from their size, though. Is there
nothing else ?'

'They appear to be much as other foot
marks.'

'Not at all. Look here! This is the
print of a right foot in the dust. Now I
make one with my naked foot beside it.
What is the chief difference ?'

'Your toes are all cramped together. The
other print has each toe distinctly divided.'

'Quite so. That is the point. Bear that

in mind. Now, would you kindly step over
to that flap-window and smell the edge of the
wood-work ? I shall stay over here, as I
have this handkerchief in my hand.'

I did as he directed, and was instantly
conscious of a strong tarry smell.

'That is where he put his foot in getting
out. If *you* can trace him, I should think
that Toby will have no difficulty. Now run
downstairs, loose the dog, and look out for
Blondin.'

By the time that I got out into the grounds
Sherlock Holmes was on the roof, and I could
see him like an enormous glow-worm crawling
very slowly along the ridge. I lost sight of
him behind a stack of chimneys, but he
presently reappeared, and then vanished once
more upon the opposite side. When I made
my way round there I found him seated at
one of the corner eaves.

'That you, Watson ?' he cried.

'Yes.'

'This is the place. What is that black thing down there ?'

'A water-barrel.'

'Top on it ?'

'Yes.'

'No sign of a ladder ?'

'No.'

'Confound the fellow! It's a most break-neck place. I ought to be able to come down where he could climb up. The water-pipe feels pretty firm. Here goes, any-how.'

There was a scuffling of feet, and the lantern began to come steadily down the side of the wall. Then with a light spring he came on to the barrel, and from there to the earth.

'It was easy to follow him,' he said, draw-ing on his stockings and boots. 'Tiles were loosened the whole way along, and in his hurry he had dropped this.   It confirms my diagnosis, as you doctors express it.'

The object which he held up to me was a small pocket or pouch woven out of coloured grasses and with a few tawdry beads strung round it.   In shape and size it was not unlike a cigarette-case.   Inside were half a dozen spines of dark wood, sharp at one end and rounded at the other, like that which had struck Bartholomew Sholto.

'They are hellish things,' said he.   'Look out that you don't prick yourself.   I'm delighted to have them, for the chances are that they are all he has.   There is the less fear of you or me finding one in our skin before long.   I would sooner face a Martini bullet, myself.   Are you game for a six-mile trudge, Watson?'

'Certainly,' I answered.

'Your leg will stand it?'

'Oh yes.'

' Here you are, doggy ! Good old Toby !
Smell it, Toby, smell it !' he pushed the
creosote handkerchief under the dog's nose,
while the creature stood with its fluffy legs
separated, and with a most comical cock to its
head, like a connoisseur sniffing the *bouquet*
of a famous vintage. Holmes then threw the
handkerchief to a distance, fastened a stout
cord to the mongrel's collar, and led him to
the foot of the water-barrel. The creature
instantly broke into a succession of high,
tremulous yelps, and, with his nose on the
ground, and his tail in the air, pattered off
upon the trail at a pace which strained his
leash and kept us at the top of our speed.

The east had been gradually whitening,
and we could now see some distance in the
cold gray light. The square, massive house,
with its black, empty windows and high, bare
walls, towered up, sad and forlorn, behind
us. Our course led right across the grounds,

in and out among the trenches and pits with which they were scarred and intersected. The whole place. with its scattered dirt-heaps and ill-grown shrubs, had a blighted, ill-omened look which harmonized with the black tragedy which hung over it.

On reaching the boundary wall Toby ran along, whining eagerly, underneath its shadow, and stopped finally in a corner screened by a young beech. Where the two walls joined, several bricks had been loosened, and the crevices left were worn down and rounded upon the lower side, as though they had frequently been used as a ladder. Holmes clambered up, and, taking the dog from me, he dropped it over upon the other side.

'There's the print of wooden-leg's hand,' he remarked, as I mounted up beside him. 'You see the slight smudge of blood upon the white plaster. What a lucky thing it is that we have had no very heavy rain since yesterday ! The scent will lie upon the road in spite of their eight-and-twenty hours' start.'

I confess that I had my doubts myself when I reflected upon the great traffic which had passed along the London road in the interval. My fears were soon appeased, however. Toby never hesitated or swerved, but waddled on in his peculiar rolling fashion. Clearly, the pungent smell of the creasote rose high above all other contending scents.

'Do not imagine,' said Holmes, 'that I depend for my success in this case upon the mere chance of one of these fellows having put his foot in the chemical. I have knowledge now which would enable me to trace them in many different ways. This, however, is the readiest, and, since fortune has put it into our hands, I should be culpable if I neglected it. It has, however, prevented the case from becoming the pretty little

intellectual problem which it at one time
promised to be. There might have been
some credit to be gained out of it, but for
this too palpable clue.'

'There is credit, and to spare,' said I.
'I assure you, Holmes, that I marvel at the
means by which you obtain your results in
this case, even more than I did in the
Jefferson Hope murder. The thing seems
to me to be deeper and more inexplicable.
How, for example, could you describe with
such confidence the wooden-legged man?'

'Pshaw, my dear boy! it was simplicity
itself. I don't wish to be theatrical. It is
all patent and above-board. Two officers
who are in command of a convict-guard learn
an important secret as to buried treasure. A
map is drawn for them by an Englishman
named Jonathan Small. You remember that
we saw the name upon the chart in Captain
Morstan's possession. He had signed it in

behalf of himself and his associates—the sign
of the four, as he somewhat dramatically
called it. Aided by this chart, the officers—
or one of them—gets the treasure and brings
it to England, leaving, we will suppose, some
condition under which he received it un-
fulfilled. Now, then, why did not Jonathan
Small get the treasure himself ? The answer
is obvious. The chart is dated at a time
when Morstan was brought into close associ-
ation with convicts. Jonathan Small did not
get the treasure because he and his associates
were themselves convicts and could not get
away.'

' But this is mere speculation,' said I.

' It is more than that. It is the only
hypothesis which covers the facts. Let us
see how it fits in with the sequel. Major
Sholto remains at peace for some years,
happy in the possession of his treasure.
Then he receives a etter from India which

gives him a great fright. What was that ?'

'A letter to say that the men whom he had wronged had been set free.'

'Or had escaped. That is much more likely, for he would have known what their term of imprisonment was. It would not have been a surprise to him. What does he do then ? He guards himself against a wooden-legged man—a white man, mark you, for he mistakes a white tradesman for him, and actually fires a pistol at him. Now, only one white man's name is on the chart. The others are Hindoos or Mohammedans. There is no other white man. Therefore we may say with confidence that the wooden-legged man is identical with Jonathan Small. Does the reasoning strike you as being faulty ?'

'No: it is clear and concise.'

'Well, now, let us put ourselves in the

place of Jonathan Small. Let us look at it from his point of view. He comes to England with the double idea of regaining what he would consider to be his rights and of having his revenge upon the man who had wronged him. He found out where Sholto lived, and very possibly he established communications with some one inside the house. There is this butler, Lal Rao, whom we have not seen. Mrs. Bernstone gives him far from a good character. Small could not find out, however, where the treasure was hid, for no one ever knew, save the major and one faithful servant who had died. Suddenly Small learns that the major is on his death-bed. In a frenzy lest the secret of the treasure die with him, he runs the gauntlet of the guards, makes his way to the dying man's window, and is only deterred from entering by the presence of his two sons. Mad with hate, however, against the dead

9

man, he enters the room that night, searches his private papers in the hope of discovering some memorandum relating to the treasure, and finally leaves a memento of his visit in the short inscription upon the card.   He had doubtless planned beforehand that, should he slay the major, he would leave some such record upon the body as a sign that it was not a common murder, but, from the point of view of the four associates, something in the nature of an act of justice.   Whimsical and bizarre conceits of this kind are common enough in the annals of crime, and usually afford valuable indications as to the criminal. Do you follow all this ?'

' Very clearly.'

' Now, what could Jonathan Small do ? He could only continue to keep a secret watch upon the efforts made to find the treasure.   Possibly he leaves England and only comes back at intervals.   Then comes

the discovery of the garret, and he is instantly informed of it. We again trace the
presence of some confederate in the house-
hold. Jonathan, with his wooden leg, is
utterly unable to reach the lofty room of
Bartholomew Sholto. He takes with him,
however, a rather curious associate, who gets
over this difficulty, but dips his naked foot
into creosote, whence come Toby, and a six-
mile limp for a half-pay officer with a
damaged tendo Achillis.'

'But it was the associate, and not Jonathan,
who committed the crime.'

'Quite so. And rather to Jonathan's disgust, to judge by the way he stamped about
when he got into the room. He bore no
grudge against Bartholomew Sholto, and
would have preferred if he could have been
simply bound and gagged. He did not wish
to put his head in a halter. There was no
help for it, however : the savage instincts of

his companion had broken out, and the poison had done its work : so Jonathan Small left his record, lowered the treasure-box to the ground, and followed it himself. That was the train of events as far as I can decipher them. Of course as to his personal appearance he must be middle-aged, and must be sunburned after serving his time in such an oven as the Andamans. His height is readily calculated from the length of his stride, and we know that he was bearded. His hairiness was the one point which impressed itself upon Thaddeus Sholto when he saw him at the window. I don't know that there is anything else.'

' The associate ?'

'Ah, well, there is no great mystery in that. But you will know all about it soon enough. How sweet the morning air is ! See how that one little cloud floats like a pink feather from some gigantic flamingo.

Now the red rim of the sun pushes itself over
the London cloud-bank.   It shines on a good
many folk, but on none, I dare bet, who are
on a stranger errand than you and I.   How
small we feel with our petty ambitions and
strivings in the presence of the great ele-
mental forces of nature!   Are you well up
in your Jean Paul?'

'Fairly so.   I worked back to him through
Carlyle.'

'That was like following the brook to the
parent lake.   He makes one curious but
profound remark.   It is that the chief proof
of man's real greatness lies in his perception
of his own smallness.   It argues, you see, a
power of comparison and of appreciation
which is in itself a proof of nobility.   There
is much food for thought in Richter.   You
have not a pistol, have you?'

'I have my stick.'

'It is just possible that we may need

something of the sort if we get to their lair. Jonathan I shall leave to you, but if the other turns nasty I shall shoot him dead.'

He took out his revolver as he spoke, and, having loaded two of the chambers, he put it back into the right-hand pocket of his jacket.

We had during this time been following the guidance of Toby down the half-rural villa-lined roads which lead to the metropolis. Now, however, we were beginning to come among continuous streets, where labourers and dockmen were already astir, and slatternly women were taking down shutters and brushing door-steps. At the square-topped corner public-houses business was just beginning, and rough-looking men were emerging, rubbing their sleeves across their beards after their morning wet. Strange dogs sauntered up and stared wonderingly at us as we passed, but our inimitable Toby

looked neither to the right or to the left, but
trotted onwards with his nose to the ground
and an occasional eager whine which spoke
of a hot scent.

We had traversed Streatham, Brixton,
Camberwell, and now found ourselves in
Kennington Lane, having borne away
through the side streets to the east of the
Oval. The men whom we pursued seemed
to have taken a curiously zigzag road, with
the idea probably of escaping observation.
They had never kept to the main road if a
parallel side-street would serve their turn.
At the foot of Kennington Lane they had
edged away to the left through Bond Street
and Miles Street. Where the latter street
turns into Knight's Place, Toby ceased to
advance, but began to run backwards and
forwards with one ear cocked and the other
drooping, the very picture of canine inde-
cision. Then he waddled round in circles,

looking up to us from time to time, as if to ask for sympathy in his embarrassment.

'What the deuce is the matter with the dog?' growled Holmes. 'They surely would not take a cab, or go off in a balloon.'

'Perhaps they stood here for some time,' I suggested.

'Ah! it's all right. He's off again,' said my companion, in a tone of relief.

He was indeed off, for after sniffing round again he suddenly made up his mind, and darted away with an energy and determination such as he had not yet shown. The scent appeared to be much hotter than before, for he had not even to put his nose on the ground, but tugged at his leash and tried to break into a run. I could see by the gleam in Holmes's eyes that he thought we were nearing the end of our journey.

Our course now ran down Nine Elms until we came to Broderick and Nelson's large timber-yard, just past the White Eagle tavern. Here the dog, frantic with excitement, turned down through the side gate into the enclosure, where the sawyers were already at work. On the dog raced through sawdust and shavings, down an alley, round a passage, between two wood-piles, and finally, with a triumphant yelp, sprang upon a large barrel which still stood upon the hand-trolley on which it had been brought. With lolling tongue and blinking eyes, Toby stood upon the cask, looking from one to the other of us for some sign of appreciation. The staves of the barrel and the wheels of the trolley were smeared with a dark liquid, and the whole air was heavy with the smell of creosote.

Sherlock Holmes and I looked blankly at each other, and then burst simultaneously into an uncontrollable fit of laughter.

CHAPTER VIII.

THE BAKER STREET IRREGULARS.

'WHAT now?' I asked. 'Toby has lost his character for infallibility.'

'He acted according to his lights,' said Holmes, lifting him down from the barrel and walking him out of the timber-yard. 'If you consider how much creosote is carted about London in one day, it is no great wonder that our trail should have been crossed. It is much used now, especially for the seasoning of wood. Poor Toby is not to blame.'

'We must get on the main scent again, I suppose.'

'Yes. And, fortunately, we have no

distance to go. Evidently what puzzled the dog at the corner of Knight's Place was that there were two different trails running in opposite directions. We took the wrong one. It only remains to follow the other.'

There was no difficulty about this. On leading Toby to the place where he had committed his fault, he cast about in a wide circle and finally dashed off in a fresh direction.

'We must take care that he does not now bring us to the place where the creosote-barrel came from,' I observed.

'I had thought of that. But you notice that he keeps on the pavement, whereas the barrel passed down the roadway. No, we are on the true scent now.'

It tended down towards the river-side, running through Belmont Place and Prince's Street. At the end of Broad Street it ran right down to the water's edge, where there was a small wooden wharf. Toby led us to the very edge of this, and there stood whining, looking out on the dark current beyond.

'We are out of luck,' said Holmes. 'They have taken to a boat here.'

Several small punts and skiffs were lying about in the water and on the edge of the wharf. We took Toby round to each in turn, but, though he sniffed earnestly, he made no sign.

Close to the rude landing-stage was a small brick house, with a wooden placard slung out through the second window. 'Mordecai Smith' was printed across it in large letters, and, underneath, 'Boats to hire by the hour or day.' A second inscription above the door informed us that a steam launch was kept—a statement which was confirmed by a great pile of coke upon the jetty. Sherlock Holmes looked slowly round, and his face assumed an ominous expression.

'This looks bad,' said he. 'These fellows are sharper than I expected. They seem to have covered their tracks. There has, I fear, been preconcerted management here.'

He was approaching the door of the house, when it opened, and a little curly-headed lad of six came running out, followed by a stoutish, red-faced woman with a large sponge in her hand.

'You come back and be washed, Jack,' she shouted. 'Come back, you young imp; for if your father comes home and finds you like that, he'll let us hear of it.'

'Dear little chap!' said Holmes strategically. 'What a rosy-cheeked young rascal! Now, Jack, is there anything you would like?'

The youth pondered for a moment.

'I'd like a shillin',' said he.

'Nothing you would like better?'

'I'd like two shillin' better,' the prodigy answered, after some thought.

Here you are, then! Catch!—A fine child, Mrs. Smith!'

'Lor' bless you, sir, he is that, and forward. He gets a'most too much for me to manage, 'specially when my man is away days at a time.'

'Away, is he?' said Holmes, in a disappointed voice. 'I am sorry for that, for I wanted to speak to Mr. Smith.'

'He's been away since yesterday mornin', sir, and, truth to tell, I am beginnin' to feel frightened about him. But if it was about a boat, sir, maybe I could serve as well.'

'I wanted to hire his steam launch.'

'Why, bless you, sir, it is in the steam launch that he has gone. That's what puzzles me; for I know there ain't more coals in her than would take her to about Woolwich and back. If he'd been away in the barge I'd ha' thought nothin'; for many a time a job has taken him as far as Graves-

end, and then if there was much doin' there
he might ha' stayed over. But what good
is a steam launch without coals ?'

'He might have bought some at a wharf
down the river.'

'He might, sir, but it weren't his way.
Many a time I've heard him call out at the
prices they charge for a few odd bags. Besides, I don't like that wooden-legged man,
wi' his ugly face and outlandish talk. What
did he want always knockin' about here for ?'

'A wooden-legged man ?' said Holmes,
with bland surprise.

'Yes, sir, a brown, monkey-faced chap
that's called more'n once for my old man.
It was him that roused him up yesternight,
and, what's more, my man knew he was
comin', for he had steam up in the launch.
I tell you straight, sir, I don't feel easy in
my mind about it.'

'But, my dear Mrs. Smith,' said Holmes,

shrugging his shoulders, ' you are frightening yourself about nothing. How could you possibly tell that it was the wooden-legged man who came in the night? I don't quite understand how you can be so sure.'

' His voice, sir. I knew his voice, which is kind o' thick and foggy. He tapped at the winder—about three it would be. " Show a leg, matey," says he : " time to turn out guard." My old man woke up Jim—that's my eldest—and away they went, without so much as a word to me. I could hear the wooden leg clackin' on the stones.'

' And was this wooden-legged man alone ?'

'Couldn't say, I am sure, sir. I didn't hear no one else.'

' I am sorry, Mrs. Smith, for I wanted a steam launch, and I have heard good reports of the—— Let me see, what is her name ?'

' The *Aurora,* sir.

'Ah! She's not that old green launch with a yellow line, very broad in the beam?

· No, indeed. She's as trim a little thing as any on the river. She's been fresh painted, black with two red streaks.'

' Thanks. I hope that you will hear soon from Mr. Smith. I am going down the river, and if I should see anything of the *Aurora* I shall let him know that you are uneasy. A black funnel, you say?'

' No, sir. Black with a white band.'

' Ah, of course. It was the sides which were black. Good-morning, Mrs. Smith. There is a boatman here with a wherry, Watson. We shall take it and cross the river.

' The main thing with people of that sort,' said Holmes, as we sat in the sheets of the wherry, ' is never to let them think that their information can be of the slightest import-ance to you. If you do, they will instantly shut up like an oyster. Ii you listen to them

10

under protest, as it were, you are very likely
to get what you want.'

'Our course now seems pretty clear,'
said I.

'What would you do. then?'

'I would engage a launch and go down
the river on the track of the *Aurora.*'

'My dear fellow, it would be a colossal
task.   She may have touched at any wharf
on either side of the stream between here
and Greenwich.   Below the bridge there is
a perfect labyrinth of landing-places for
miles.   It would take you days and days to
exhaust them, if you set about it alone.'

'Employ the police, then.'

'No.   I shall probably call Athelney
Jones in at the last moment.   He is not a
bad fellow, and I should not like to do anything which would injure him professionally.
But I have a fancy for working it out myself,
now that we have gone so far.'

'Could we advertise, then, asking for information from wharfingers?'

'Worse and worse! Our men would know that the chase was hot at their heels, and they would be off out of the country As it is, they are likely enough to leave, but as long as they think they are perfectly safe they will be in no hurry. Jones's energy will be of use to us there, for his view of the case is sure to push itself into the daily press, and the runaways will think that everyone is off on the wrong scent.'

'What are we to do, then?' I asked, as we landed near Millbank Penitentiary.

'Take this hansom, drive home, have some breakfast, and get an hour's sleep. It is quite on the cards that we may be afoot to-night again. Stop at a telegraph office, cabby! We will keep Toby, for he may be of use to us yet.'

We pulled up at the Great Peter Street

10—2

post-office, and Holmes despatched his wire.

'Whom do you think that is to?' he asked, as we resumed our journey.

'I am sure I don't know.'

'You remember the Baker Street division of the detective police force whom I employed in the Jefferson Hope case?'

'Well,' said I, laughing.

'This is just the case where they might be invaluable. If they fail, I have other resources; but I shall try them first. That wire was to my dirty little lieutenant, Wiggins, and I expect that he and his gang will be with us before we have finished our breakfast.'

It was between eight and nine o'clock now, and I was conscious of a strong reaction after the successive excitements of the night. I was limp and weary, befogged in mind and fatigued in body. I had not the professional enthusiasm which carried my companion on, nor could I look at the matter as a mere abstract intellectual problem. As far as the death of Bartholomew Sholto went, I had heard little good of him, and could feel no intense antipathy to his murderers. The treasure, however, was a different matter. That, or part of it, belonged rightfully to Miss Morstan. While there was a chance of recovering it I was ready to devote my life to the one object. True, if I found it, it would probably put her for ever beyond my reach. Yet it would be a petty and selfish love which would be influenced by such a thought as that. If Holmes could work to find the criminals, I had a tenfold stronger reason to urge me on to find the treasure.

A bath at Baker Street and a complete change freshened me up wonderfully. When I came down to our room I found the breakfast laid and Holmes pouring out the coffee.

' Here it is,' said he, laughing and pointing

to an open newspaper. 'The energetic Jones and the ubiquitous reporter have fixed it up between them. But you have had enough of the case. Better have your ham and eggs first.'

I took the paper from him and read the short notice, which was headed 'Mysterious Business at Upper Norwood.'

'About twelve o'clock last night,' said the *Standard*, 'Mr. Bartholomew Sholto, of Pondicherry Lodge, Upper Norwood, was found dead in his room under circumstances which point to foul play. As far as we can learn, no actual traces of violence were found upon Mr. Sholto's person, but a valuable collection of Indian gems which the deceased gentleman had inherited from his father has been carried off. The discovery was first made by Mr. Sherlock Holmes and Dr. Watson, who had called at the house with Mr. Thaddeus Sholto, brother of the deceased. By a singular piece of good fortune, Mr. Athelney Jones, the well-known member of the detective police force, happened to be at the Norwood Police Station, and was on the ground within half an hour of the first alarm. His trained and experienced faculties were at once directed towards the detection of the criminals, with the gratifying result that the brother, Thaddeus Sholto, has already been arrested, together with the housekeeper, Mrs. Bernstone, an Indian butler named Lal Rao, and a porter, or gatekeeper, named McMurdo. It is quite certain that the thief or thieves were well acquainted with the house, for Mr. Jones's well-known technical knowledge and his powers of minute observation have enabled him to prove conclusively that the miscreants could not have entered by the door or by the window, but must have made their way across the roof of the building, and so through a trap-door into a room which communicated with that in which the body was found. This fact, which has been very clearly made out, proves conclusively that it was no mere haphazard burglary. The prompt and energetic action of the officers of the law shows the great advantage of the presence on such occasions of a single vigorous and masterful mind. We cannot but think that it supplies an argument to those who would wish to see our detectives more decentralized, and so brought into closer and more effective touch with the cases which it is their duty to investigate.'

'Isn't it gorgeous!' said Holmes, grinning over his coffee cup. 'What do you think of it?'

'I think that we have had a close shave ourselves of being arrested for the crime.'

'So do I. I wouldn't answer for our safety now, if he should happen to have another of his attacks of energy.'

At this moment there was a loud ring at the bell, and I could hear Mrs. Hudson, our landlady, raising her voice in a wail of expostulation and dismay.

' By heavens, Holmes,' I said, half rising, ' I believe that they are really after us.'

' No, it's not quite so bad as that. It is the unofficial force—the Baker Street irregulars.'

As he spoke, there came a swift pattering of naked feet upon the stairs, a clatter of high voices, and in rushed a dozen dirty and ragged little street Arabs. There was some show of discipline among them, despite their tumultuous entry, for they instantly drew up in line and stood facing us with expectant faces. One of their number, taller and older than the others, stood forward with an air of lounging superiority which was very funny in such a disreputable little scarecrow

'Got your message, sir,' said he, 'and brought 'em on sharp. Three bob and a tanner for tickets.'

'Here you are,' said Holmes, producing some silver. 'In future they can report to you, Wiggins, and you to me. I cannot have the house invaded in this way. However, it is just as well that you should all hear the instructions. I want to find the whereabouts of a steam launch called the *Aurora*, owner Mordecai Smith, black with two red streaks, funnel black with a white band. She is down the river somewhere. I want one boy to be at Mordecai Smith's landing-stage opposite Millbank to say if the boat comes back. You must divide it out among yourselves, and do both banks thoroughly. Let me know the moment you have news. Is that all clear?'

'Yes, guv'nor,' said Wiggins.

' The old scale of pay, and a guinea to the

boy who finds the boat. Here's a day in
advance. Now off you go!'

He handed them a shilling each, and away
they buzzed down the stairs, and I saw them
a moment later streaming down the street.

' If the launch is above water they will find
her,' said Holmes, as he rose from the table
and lit his pipe. ' They can go everywhere,
see everything, overhear everyone. I expect
to hear before evening that they have spotted
her. In the meanwhile, we can do nothing
but await results. We cannot pick up the
broken trail until we find either the *Aurora*
or Mr. Mordecai Smith.'

' Toby could eat these scraps, I dare say.
Are you going to bed, Holmes ?'

'No : I am not tired. I have a curious
constitution. I never remember feeling tired
by work, though idleness exhausts me completely. I am going to smoke and to think
over this queer business to which my fair

client has introduced us. If ever man had an
easy task, this of ours ought to be. Wooden-
legged men are not so common, but the other
man must, I should think, be absolutely
unique.'

'That other man again !'

'I have no wish to make a mystery of him
to you, anyway. But you must have formed
your own opinion. Now, do consider the
data. Diminutive footmarks, toes never
fettered by boots, naked feet, stone-headed
wooden mace, great agility, small poisoned
darts. What do you make of all this ?'

'A savage !' I exclaimed. 'Perhaps one of
those Indians who were the associates of
Jonathan Small.'

'Hardly that,' said he. 'When first I saw
signs of strange weapons, I was inclined to
think so ; but the remarkable character of the
footmarks caused me to reconsider my views.
Some of the inhabitants of the Indian Penin-

sula are small men, but none could have left such marks as that. The Hindoo proper has long and thin feet. The sandal-wearing Mohammedan has the great toe well separated from the others, because the thong is commonly passed between. These little darts, too, could only be shot in one way. They are from a blow-pipe. Now, then, where are we to find our savage?'

'South American,' I hazarded.

He stretched his hand up, and took down a bulky volume from the shelf.

'This is the first volume of a gazetteer which is now being published. It may be looked upon as the very latest authority. What have we here? "Andaman Islands, situated 340 miles to the north of Sumatra, in the Bay of Bengal." Hum! hum! What's all this? Moist climate, coral reefs, sharks, Port Blair, convict barracks, Rutland Island, cottonwoods—— Ah, here we are! "The

aborigines of the Andaman Islands may perhaps claim the distinction of being the smallest
race upon this earth, though some anthro-
pologists prefer the Bushmen of Africa, the
Digger Indians of America, and the Terra
del Fuegians.   The average height is rather
below four feet, although many full-grown
adults may be found who are very much
smaller than this.   They are a fierce, morose,
and intractable people, though capable of
forming most devoted friendships when their
confidence has once been gained."   Mark
that, Watson.   Now, then, listen to this.
" They are naturally hideous, having large,
misshapen heads, small fierce eyes, and distorted features.   Their feet and hands, however, are remarkably small.   So intractable
and fierce are they, that all the efforts of the
British officials have failed to win them over
in any degree.   They have always been a
terror to shipwrecked crews, braining the

survivors with their stone-headed clubs, or shooting them with their poisoned arrows. These massacres are invariably concluded by a cannibal feast." Nice, amiable people, Watson! If this fellow had been left to his own unaided devices, this affair might have taken an even more ghastly turn. I fancy that, even as it is, Jonathan Small would give a good deal not to have employed him.'

'But how came he to have so singular a companion?'

'Ah, that is more than I can tell. Since, however, we had already determined that Small had come from the Andamans, it is not so very wonderful that this islander should be with him. No doubt we shall know all about it in time. Look here, Watson; you look regularly done. Lie down there on the sofa, and see if I can put you to sleep.'

He took up his violin from the corner, and as I stretched myself out he began to play some low, dreamy, melodious air—his own, no doubt, for he had a remarkable gift for improvisation. I have a vague remembrance of his gaunt limbs, his earnest face, and the rise and fall of his bow. Then I seemed to be floated peacefully away upon a soft sea of sound, until I found myself in dreamland, with the sweet face of Mary Morstan looking down upon me.

CHAPTER IX.

A BREAK IN THE CHAIN.

IT was late in the afternoon before I woke, strengthened and refreshed. Sherlock Holmes still sat exactly as I had left him, save that he had laid aside his violin and was deep in a book. He looked across at me as I stirred, and I noticed that his face was dark and troubled.

'You have slept soundly,' he said. 'I feared that our talk would wake you.'

'I heard nothing,' I answered. 'Have you had fresh news, then?'

'Unfortunately, no. I confess that I am surprised and disappointed. I expected something definite by this time. Wiggins has

11

just been up to report. He says that no trace can be found of the launch. It is a provoking check, for every hour is of importance.'

'Can I do anything ? I am perfectly fresh now, and quite ready for another night's outing.'

'No ; we can do nothing. We can only wait. If we go ourselves, the message might come in our absence, and delay be caused. You can do what you will, but I must remain on guard.'

'Then I shall run over to Camberwell and call upon Mrs. Cecil Forrester. She asked me to, yesterday.'

'On Mrs. Cecil Forrester ?' asked Holmes, with the twinkle of a smile in his eyes.

'Well, of course on Miss Morstan too. They were anxious to hear what happened.'

'I would not tell them too much,' said

Holmes. 'Women are never to be entirely trusted—not the best of them.'

I did not pause to argue over this atrocious sentiment.

'I shall be back in an hour or two,' I remarked.

'All right! Good luck! But, I say, if you are crossing the river you may as well return Toby, for I don't think it is at all likely that we shall have any use for him now.'

I took our mongrel accordingly, and left him, together with a half-sovereign, at the old naturalist's in Pinchin Lane. At Camberwell I found Miss Morstan a little weary after her night's adventures, but very eager to hear the news. Mrs. Forrester, too, was full of curiosity. I told them all that we had done, suppressing, however, the more dreadful parts of the tragedy. Thus, although I spoke of Mr. Sholto's death, I said nothing of the exact manner and method of it. With all my omissions, however, there was enough to startle and amaze them.

'It is a romance!' cried Mrs. Forrester. 'An injured lady, half a million in treasure, a black cannibal, and a wooden-legged ruffian. They take the place of the conventional dragon or wicked earl.'

'And two knight-errants to the rescue,' added Miss Morstan, with a bright glance at me.

'Why, Mary, your fortune depends upon the issue of this search. I don't think that you are nearly excited enough. Just imagine what it must be to be so rich, and to have the world at your feet!'

It sent a little thrill of joy to my heart to notice that she showed no sign of elation at the prospect. On the contrary, she gave a toss of her proud head, as though the matter were one in which she took small interest.

'It is for Mr. Thaddeus Sholto that I am anxious,' she said. 'Nothing else is of any consequence ; but I think that he has behaved most kindly and honourably through-out. It is our duty to clear him of this dreadful and unfounded charge.'

It was evening before I left Camberwell, and quite dark by the time I reached home. My companion's book and pipe lay by his chair, but he had disappeared. I looked about in the hope of seeing a note, but there was none.

'I suppose that Mr. Sherlock Holmes has gone out,' I said to Mrs. Hudson as she came up to lower the blinds.

'No, sir. He has gone to his room, sir. Do you know, sir,' sinking her voice into an impressive whisper, 'I am afraid for his health ?'

'Why so, Mrs. Hudson?'

'Well, he's that strange, sir. After you was gone he walked and he walked, up and down, and up and down, until I was weary of the sound of his footstep. Then I heard him talking to himself and muttering, and every time the bell rang out he came on the stair-head, with "What is that, Mrs. Hudson?" And now he has slammed off to his room, but I can hear him walking away the same as ever. I hope he's not going to be ill, sir. I ventured to say something to him about cooling medicine, but he turned on me, sir, with such a look that I don't know how ever I got out of the room.'

'I don't think that you have any cause to be uneasy, Mrs. Hudson,' I answered. 'I have seen him like this before. He has some small matter upon his mind which makes him restless.'

I tried to speak lightly to our worthy

landlady, but I was myself somewhat uneasy when through the long night I still
from time to time heard the dull sound of
his tread, and knew how his keen spirit was
chafing against this involuntary inaction.

At breakfast-time he looked worn and
haggard, with a little fleck of feverish colour
upon either cheek.

'You are knocking yourself up, old man,'
I remarked. 'I heard you marching about
in the night.'

'No, I could not sleep,' he answered.
'This infernal problem is consuming me.
It is too much to be baulked by so petty
an obstacle, when all else had been over-
come. I know the men, the launch, everything; and yet I can get no news. I have
set other agencies at work, and used every
means at my disposal. The whole river has
been searched on either side, but there is
no news, nor has Mrs. Smith heard of her

husband. I shall come to the conclusion soon that they have scuttled the craft. But there are objections to that.'

'Or that Mrs. Smith has put us on a wrong scent.'

'No, I think that may be dismissed. I had inquiries made, and there is a launch of that description.'

'Could it have gone up the river?'

'I have considered that possibility too, and there is a search-party who will work up as far as Richmond. If no news comes to-day, I shall start off myself to-morrow, and go for the men rather than the boat. But surely, surely, we shall hear something.'

We did not, however. Not a word came to us either from Wiggins or from the other agencies. There were articles in most of the papers upon the Norwood tragedy. They all appeared to be rather hostile to the unfortunate Thaddeus Sholto. No fresh details were to be found, however, in any of them, save that an inquest was to be held upon the following day. I walked over to Camberwell in the evening to report our ill-success to the ladies, and on my return I found Holmes dejected and somewhat morose. He would hardly reply to my questions, and busied himself all the evening in an abstruse chemical analysis which involved much heating of retorts and distilling of vapours, ending at last in a smell which fairly drove me out of the apartment. Up to the small hours of the morning I could hear the clinking of his test-tubes which told me that he was still engaged in his malodorous experiment.

In the early dawn I woke with a start, and was surprised to find him standing by my bedside, clad in a rude sailor dress with a pea-jacket, and a coarse red scarf round his neck.

'I am off down the river, Watson,' said he. 'I have been turning it over in my mind, and I can see only one way out of it. It is worth trying, at all events.'

'Surely I can come with you, then?' said I.

'No; you can be much more useful if you will remain here as my representative. I am loath to go, for it is quite on the cards that some message may come during the day, though Wiggins was despondent about it last night. I want you to open all notes and telegrams, and to act on your own judgment if any news should come. Can I rely upon you?'

'Most certainly.'

'I am afraid that you will not be able to wire to me, for I can hardly tell yet where I may find myself. If I am in luck, however, I may not be gone so very long. I shall have news of some sort or other before I get back.'

I had heard nothing of him by breakfast time. On opening the *Standard*, however, I found that there was a fresh allusion to the business. 'With reference to the Upper Norwood tragedy,' it remarked, 'we have reason to believe that the matter promises to be even more complex and mysterious than was originally supposed. Fresh evidence has shown that it is quite impossible that Mr. Thaddeus Sholto could have been in any way concerned in the matter. He and the housekeeper, Mrs. Bernstone, were both released yesterday evening. It is believed, however, that the police have a clue as to the real culprits, and that it is being prosecuted by Mr. Athelney Jones, of Scotland Yard, with all his well-known energy and sagacity. Further arrests may be expected at any moment.'

'That is satisfactory so far as it goes,' thought I. 'Friend Sholto is safe, at any rate. I wonder what the fresh clue may be, though it seems to be a stereotyped form whenever the police have made a blunder.'

I tossed the paper down upon the table, but at that moment my eye caught an advertisement in the agony column. It ran in this way :

'Lost.—Whereas Mordecai Smith, boatman, and his son Jim, left Smith's Wharf at or about three o'clock last Tuesday morning in the steam launch *Aurora*, black with two red stripes, funnel black with a white band, the sum of five pounds will be paid to anyone who can give information to Mrs. Smith, at Smith's Wharf, or at 221*b*, Baker Street, as to the whereabouts of the said Mordecai Smith and the launch *Aurora.*'

This was clearly Holmes's doing. The Baker Street address was enough to prove that. It struck me as rather ingenious, because it might be read by the fugitives without their seeing in it more than the natural anxiety of a wife for her missing husband.

It was a long day. Every time that a knock came to the door, or a sharp step passed in the street, I imagined that it was either Holmes returning or an answer to his advertisement. I tried to read, but my thoughts would wander off to our strange quest and to the ill-assorted and villainous pair whom we were pursuing. Could there be, I wondered, some radical flaw in my companion's reasoning? Might he not be suffering from some huge self-deception? Was it not possible that his nimble and speculative mind had built up this wild theory upon faulty premises? I had never known him to be wrong, and yet the keenest reasoner may occasionally be deceived. He was likely, I thought, to fall into error through the over-refinement of his logic—his pre-

ference for a subtle and bizarre explanation
when a plainer and more common-place one
lay ready to his hand.   Yet, on the other
hand, I had myself seen the evidence, and
I had heard the reasons for his deductions.
When I looked back on the long chain of
curious circumstances, many of them trivial
in themselves, but all tending in the same
direction, I could not disguise from myself
that even if Holmes's explanation were in-
correct the true theory must be equally *outré*
and startling.

At three o'clock in the afternoon there
was a loud peal at the bell, an authoritative
voice in the hall, and, to my surprise, no less
a person than Mr. Athelney Jones was
shown up to me.   Very different was he,
however, from the brusque and masterful
professor of common sense who had taken
over the case so confidently at Upper
Norwood.   His expression was downcast,

and his bearing meek and even apologetic.

'Good-day, sir ; good-day,' said he. 'Mr. Sherlock Holmes is out, I understand.'

'Yes, and I cannot be sure when he will be back. But perhaps you would care to wait. Take that chair and try one of these cigars.'

'Thank you ; I don't mind if I do,' said he, mopping his face with a red bandanna handkerchief.

'And a whisky and soda?'

'Well, half a glass. It is very hot for the time of year ; and I have had a good deal to worry and try me. You know my theory about this Norwood case?'

'I remember that you expressed one.'

'Well, I have been obliged to reconsider it. I had my net drawn tightly round Mr. Sholto, sir, when pop he went through a hole in the middle of it. He was able to prove an alibi which could not be shaken. From the time that he left his brother's room he was never out of sight of someone or other. So it could not be he who climbed over roofs and through trap-doors. It's a very dark case, and my professional credit is at stake. I should be very glad of a little assistance.'

'We all need help sometimes,' said I.

'Your friend Mr. Sherlock Holmes is a wonderful man, sir,' said he, in a husky and confidential voice. 'He's a man who is not to be beat. I have known that young man go into a good many cases, but I never saw the case yet that he could not throw a light upon. He is irregular in his methods, and a little quick perhaps in jumping at theories, but, on the whole, I think he would have made a most promising officer, and I don't care who knows it. I have had a wire from him this morning, by which I understand that he has got some clue to this Sholto business. Here is his message.'

He took the telegram out of his pocket, and handed it to me. It was dated from Poplar at twelve o'clock. 'Go to Baker Street at once,' it said. 'If I have not returned, wait for me. I am close on the track of the Sholto gang. You can come with us to-night if you want to be in at the finish.'

'This sounds well. He has evidently picked up the scent again,' said I.

'Ah, then he has been at fault too,' exclaimed Jones, with evident satisfaction. 'Even the best of us are thrown off sometimes. Of course this may prove to be a false alarm; but it is my duty as an officer of the law to allow no chance to slip. But there is someone at the door. Perhaps this is he.'

A heavy step was heard ascending the stair, with a great wheezing and rattling as from a man who was sorely put to it for

breath. Once or twice he stopped, as though
the climb were too much for him, but at last
he made his way to our door and entered.
His appearance corresponded to the sounds
which we had heard.   He was an aged man,
clad in seafaring garb, with an old pea-jacket
buttoned up to his throat. His back was
bowed, his knees were shaky, and his
breathing was painfully asthmatic. As he
leaned upon a thick oaken cudgel his
shoulders heaved in the effort to draw the
air into his lungs. He had a coloured scarf
round his chin, and I could see little of his
face save a pair of keen dark eyes, overhung
by bushy white brows, and long gray side-
whiskers. Altogether he gave me the impression of a respectable master mariner who
had fallen into years and poverty.

'What is it, my man?' I asked.

He looked about him in the slow methodical
fashion of old age.

' Is Mr. Sherlock Holmes here ?' said he.

' No ; but I am acting for him. You can tell me any message you have for him.'

' It was to him himself I was to tell it,' said he.

' But I tell you that I am acting for him. Was it about Mordecai Smith's boat ?'

' Yes. I knows well where it is. An' I knows where the men he is after are. An' I knows where the treasure is. I knows all about it.'

' Then tell me, and I shall let him know.'

' It was to him I was to tell it,' he repeated, with the petulant obstinacy of a very old man.

' Well, you must wait for him.'

' No, no ; I ain't goin' to lose a whole day to please no one. If Mr. Holmes ain't here, then Mr. Holmes must find it all out for himself. I don't care about the look of either of you, and I won't tell a word.'

He shuffled towards the door, but Athelney Jones got in front of him.

'Wait a bit, my friend,' said he. 'You have important information, and you must not walk off. We shall keep you, whether you like or not, until our friend returns.'

The old man made a little run towards the door, but, as Athelney Jones put his broad back up against it, he recognised the uselessness of resistance.

'Pretty sort o' treatment this!' he cried, stamping his stick. 'I come here to see a gentleman, and you two, who I never saw in my life, seize me and treat me in this fashion!'

'You will be none the worse,' I said. 'We shall recompense you for the loss of your time. Sit over here on the sofa, and you will not have long to wait.'

He came across sullenly enough, and seated himself with his face resting on his hands. Jones and I resumed our cigars and our talk. Suddenly, however, Holmes's voice broke in upon us.

'I think that you might offer me a cigar too,' he said.

We both started in our chairs. There was Holmes sitting close to us with an air of quiet amusement.

'Holmes!' I exclaimed. 'You here! But where is the old man?'

'Here is the old man,' said he, holding out a heap of white hair. 'Here he is— wig, whiskers, eyebrows, and all. I thought my disguise was pretty good, but I hardly expected that it would stand that test.'

'Ah, you rogue!' cried Jones, highly delighted. 'You would have made an actor and a rare one. You had the proper workhouse cough, and those weak legs of yours are worth ten pound a week. I thought I knew the glint of your eye, though. You didn't get away from us so easily, you see'

' I have been working in that get-up all day,' said he, lighting his cigar. ' You see, a good many of the criminal classes begin to know me—especially since our friend here took to publishing some of my cases : so I can only go on the war-path under some simple disguise like this. You got my wire ?'

' Yes ; that was what brought me here.'

' How has your case prospered ?'

' It has all come to nothing. I have had to release two of my prisoners, and there is no evidence against the other two.'

' Never mind. We shall give you two others in the place of them. But you must put yourself under my orders. You are welcome to all the official credit, but you must act on the lines that I point out. Is that agreed ?'

' Entirely, if you will help me to the men.'

' Well, then, in the first place I shall want a fast police-boat—a steam launch—to be at the Westminster Stairs at seven o'clock.'

'That is easily managed. There is always one about there; but I can step across the road and telephone to make sure.'

'Then I shall want two stanch men, in case of resistance.'

'There will be two or three in the boat. What else?'

'When we secure the men we shall get the treasure. I think that it would be a pleasure to my friend here to take the box round to the young lady to whom half of it rightfully belongs. Let her be the first to open it. Eh, Watson?'

'It would be a great pleasure to me.'

'Rather an irregular proceeding,' said Jones, shaking his head. 'However, the whole thing is irregular, and I suppose we must wink at it. The treasure must afterwards be handed over to the authorities until after the official investigation.'

'Certainly. That is easily managed. One

other point.   I should much like to have a
few details about this matter from the lips of
Jonathan Small himself.   You know I like to
work the details of my cases out.   There is
no objection to my having an unofficial interview with him, either here in my rooms or else-
where, as long as he is efficiently guarded ?'

'Well, you are master of the situation.   I
have had no proof yet of the existence of this
Jonathan Small.   However, if you can catch
him, I don't see how I can refuse you an
interview with him.'

'That is understood, then ?'

'Perfectly.   Is there anything else ?'

'Only that I insist upon your dining with
us.   It will be ready in half an hour.   I have
oysters and a brace of grouse, with something
a little choice in white wines.—Watson, you
have never yet recognized my merits as a
housekeeper.'

CHAPTER X.

THE END OF THE ISLANDER.

OUR meal was a merry one. Holmes could talk exceedingly well when he chose, and that night he did choose. He appeared to be in a state of nervous exaltation. I have never known him so brilliant. He spoke on a quick succession of subjects—on miracle plays, on mediæval pottery, on Stradivarius violins, on the Buddhism of Ceylon, and on the war-ships of the future—handling each as though he had made a special study of it. His bright humour marked the reaction from his black depression of the preceding days. Athelney Jones proved to be a sociable soul in his hours of relaxation, and faced his dinner with

the air of a *bon vivant*. For myself, I felt
elated at the thought that we were nearing the
end of our task, and I caught something of
Holmes's gaiety. None of us alluded during
dinner to the cause which had brought us
together.

When the cloth was cleared, Holmes
glanced at his watch, and filled up three
glasses with port.

'One bumper,' said he, 'to the success of
our little expedition. And now it is high
time we were off. Have you a pistol,
Watson?'

'I have my old service-revolver in my
desk.'

'You had best take it, then. It is well to
be prepared. I see that the cab is at the
door. I ordered it for half-past six.'

It was a little past seven before we reached
the Westminster wharf, and found our launch
awaiting us. Holmes eyed it critically.

'Is there anything to mark it as a police-boat ?'

'Yes, that green lamp at the side.'

'Then take it off.'

The small change was made, we stepped on board, and the ropes were cast off. Jones, Holmes, and I sat in the stern. There was one man at the rudder, one to tend the engines, and two burly police-inspectors forward.

'Where to ?' asked Jones.

'To the Tower. Tell them to stop opposite to Jacobson's Yard.'

Our craft was evidently a very fast one. We shot past the long lines of loaded barges as though they were stationary. Holmes smiled with satisfaction as we overhauled a river steamer and left her behind us.

'We ought to be able to catch anything on the river,' he said.

'Well, hardly that. But there are not many launches to beat us.'

'We shall have to catch the *Aurora*, and she has a name for being a clipper. I will tell you how the land lies, Watson. You recollect how annoyed I was at being baulked by so small a thing?'

'Yes.'

'Well, I gave my mind a thorough rest by plunging into a chemical analysis. One of our greatest statesmen has said that a change of work is the best rest. So it is. When I had succeeded in dissolving the hydrocarbon which I was at work at, I came back to our problem of the Sholtos, and thought the whole matter out again. My boys had been up the river and down the river without result. The launch was not at any landing-stage or wharf, nor had it returned. Yet it could hardly have been scuttled to hide their traces, though that always remained as a possible hypothesis if all else failed. I knew that this man Small had a certain degree of

low cunning, but I did not think him capable
of anything in the nature of delicate finesse.
That is usually a product of higher education.
I then reflected that since he had certainly
been in London some time—as we had
evidence that he maintained a continual
watch over Pondicherry Lodge—he could
hardly leave at a moment's notice, but would
need some little time, if it were only a day, to
arrange his affairs. That was the balance of
probability, at any rate.'

' It seems to me to be a little weak,' said I ;
' it is more probable that he had arranged his
affairs before ever he set out upon his
expedition.'

' No, I hardly think so. This lair of his
would be too valuable a retreat in case of
need for him to give it up until he was sure
that he could do without it. But a second
consideration struck me. Jonathan Small
must have felt that the peculiar appearance

of his companion, however much **he may** have top coated him, would give rise to gossip, and possibly be associated with this Norwood tragedy. He was quite sharp enough to see that. They had started from their headquarters under cover of darkness, and he would wish to get back before it was broad light. Now, it was past three o'clock, according to Mrs. Smith, when they got the boat. It would be quite bright, and people would be about in an hour or so. Therefore, I argued, they did not go very far. They paid Smith well to hold his tongue, reserved his launch for the final escape, and hurried to their lodgings with the treasure-box. In a couple of nights, when they had time to see what view the papers took, and whether there was any suspicion, they would make their way under cover of darkness to some ship at Gravesend or in the Downs, where no doubt they had already arranged for passages to America or the Colonies.'

'But the launch? They could not have taken that to their lodgings.'

'Quite so. I argued that the launch must be no great way off, in spite of its invisibility. I then put myself in the place of Small, and looked at it as a man of his capacity would. He would probably consider that to send back the launch or to keep it at a wharf would make pursuit easy if the police did happen to get on his track. How, then, could he conceal the launch and yet have her at hand when wanted? I wondered what I should do myself if I were in his shoes. I could only think of one way of doing it. I might hand the launch over to some boat-builder or repairer, with directions to make a trifling change in her. She would then be removed to his shed or yard, and so be effectually concealed, while at the

same time I could have her at a few hours'
notice.'

' That seems simple enough.'

' It is just these very simple things which
are extremely liable to be overlooked. However, I determined to act on the idea. I
started at once in this harmless seaman's rig
and inquired at all the yards down the river.
I drew blank at fifteen, but at the sixteenth
—Jacobson's—I learned that the *Aurora*
had been handed over to them two days ago
by a wooden-legged man, with some trivial
directions as to her rudder. " There ain't
naught amiss with her rudder," said the
foreman.   " There she lies, with the red
streaks."   At that moment who should come
down but Mordecai Smith, the missing
owner ?   He was rather the worse for liquor.
I should not, of course, have known him, but
he bellowed out his name and the name of
his launch.   " I want her to-night at eight

o'clock," said he—"eight o'clock sharp, mind, for I have two gentlemen who won't be kept waiting." They had evidently paid him well, for he was very flush of money, chucking shillings about to the men. I followed him some distance, but he subsided into an alehouse; so I went back to the yard, and, happening to pick up one of my boys on the way, I stationed him as a sentry over the launch. He is to stand at the water's edge and wave his handkerchief to us when they start. We shall be lying off in the stream, and it will be a strange thing if we do not take men, treasure, and all.'

'You have planned it all very neatly, whether they are the right men or not,' said Jones; 'but if the affair were in my hands I should have had a body of police in Jacobson's Yard, and arrested them when they came down.'

'Which would have been never. This man

13

Small is a pretty shrewd fellow. He would send a scout on ahead, and if anything made him suspicious he would lie snug for another week.'

'But you might have stuck to Mordecai Smith, and so been led to their hiding-place,' said I.

'In that case I should have wasted my day. I think that it is a hundred to one against Smith knowing where they live. As long as he has liquor and good pay, why should he ask questions? They send him messages what to do. No, I thought over every possible course, and this is the best.'

While this conversation had been proceeding, we had been shooting the long series of bridges which span the Thames. As we passed the City the last rays of the sun were gilding the cross upon the summit of St. Paul's. It was twilight before we reached the Tower.

'That is Jacobson's Yard,' said Holmes, pointing to a bristle of masts and rigging on the Surrey side. 'Cruise gently up and down here under cover of this string of lighters.' He took a pair of night-glasses from his pocket and gazed some time at the shore. 'I see my sentry at his post,' he remarked, 'but no sign of a handkerchief.'

'Suppose we go down stream a short way and lie in wait for them,' said Jones eagerly.

We were all eager by this time, even the policemen and stokers, who had a very vague idea of what was going forward.

'We have no right to take anything for granted,' Holmes answered. 'It is certainly ten to one that they go down stream, but we cannot be certain. From this point we can see the entrance of the yard, and they can hardly see us. It will be a clear night and plenty of light. We must stay where we are.

See how the folk swarm over yonder in the gaslight.'

' They are coming from work in the yard.

'Dirty-looking rascals, but I suppose every one has some little immortal spark concealed about him.   You would not think it, to look at them.   There is no *a priori* probability about it.   A strange enigma is man !'

' Someone calls him a soul concealed in an animal,' I suggested.

'Winwood Reade is good upon the subject,' said Holmes.   ' He remarks that, while the individual man is an insoluble puzzle, in the aggregate he becomes a mathematical certainty.   You can, for example, never foretell what any one man will do, but you can say with precision what an average number will be up to.   Individuals vary, but percentages remain constant.   So says the statistician.   But do I see a handkerchief ? Surely there is a white flutter over yonder.'

'Yes, it is your boy,' I cried. 'I can see him plainly.'

'And there is the *Aurora*,' exclaimed Holmes, 'and going like the devil! Full speed ahead, engineer. Make after that launch with the yellow light. By heaven, I shall never forgive myself if she proves **to** have the heels of us!'

She had slipped unseen through the yard-entrance and passed behind two or three small craft, so that she had fairly got her speed up before we saw her. Now she was flying down the stream, near in to the shore, going at a tremendous rate. Jones looked gravely at her and shook his head.

'She is very fast,' he said. 'I doubt if we shall catch her.'

'We *must* catch her!' cried Holmes, between his teeth. 'Heap it on, stokers! Make her do all she can! If we burn the boat we must have them!'

We were fairly after her now. The furnaces roared, and the powerful engines whizzed and clanked, like a great metallic heart. Her sharp, steep prow cut through the still river - water and sent two rolling waves to right and to left of us. With every throb of the engines we sprang and quivered like a living thing. One great yellow lantern in our bows threw a long, flickering funnel of light in front of us. Right ahead a dark blur upon the water showed where the *Aurora* lay, and the swirl of white foam behind her spoke of the pace at which she was going. We flashed past barges, steamers, merchant-vessels, in and out, behind this one and round the other. Voices hailed us out of the darkness, but still the *Aurora* thundered on, and still we followed close upon her track.

'Pile it on, men, pile it on!' cried Holmes, looking down into the engine-room, while the fierce glow from below beat upon his eager, aquiline face. 'Get every pound of steam you can.'

'I think we gain a little,' said Jones, with his eyes on the *Aurora*.

'I am sure of it,' said I. 'We shall be up with her in a very few minutes.'

At that moment, however, as our evil fate would have it, a tug with three barges in tow blundered in between us. It was only by putting our helm hard down that we avoided a collision, and before we could round them and recover our way the *Aurora* had gained a good two hundred yards. She was still, however, well in view, and the murky, un-certain twilight was settling into a clear, starlit night. Our boilers were strained to their utmost, and the frail shell vibrated and creaked with the fierce energy which was driving us along. We had shot through the pool, past the West India Docks, down the long Deptford Reach, and up again after rounding the Isle of Dogs. The dull blur in front of us resolved itself now clearly enough into the dainty *Aurora*. Jones turned our search light upon her, so that we could plainly see the figures upon her deck. One man sat by the stern, with something black between his knees, over which he stooped. Beside him lay a dark mass, which looked like a Newfoundland dog. The boy held the tiller, while against the red glare of the furnace I could see old Smith, stripped to the waist, and shovelling coals for dear life. They may have had some doubt at first as to whether we were really pursuing them, but now as we followed every winding and turning which they took there could no longer be any question about it. At Greenwich we were about three hundred paces behind them. At Blackwall we could not have been more than two hundred and fifty. I have coursed

many creatures in many countries during my
chequered career, but never did sport give me
such a wild thrill as this mad, flying man-
hunt down the Thames. Steadily we drew
in upon them, yard by yard. In the silence
of the night we could hear the panting and
clanking of their machinery. The man in
the stern still crouched upon the deck, and
his arms were moving as though he were
busy, while every now and then he would
look up and measure with a glance the distance which still separated us. Nearer we
came and nearer. Jones yelled to them to
stop. We were not more than four boat's-
lengths behind them, both boats flying at a
tremendous pace. It was a clear reach of the
river, with Barking Level upon one side and
the melancholy Plumstead Marshes upon the
other. At our hail the man in the stern
sprang up from the deck and shook his two
clenched fists at us, cursing the while in a

high, cracked voice. He was a good-sized, powerful man, and as he stood poising himself with legs astride, I could see that from the thigh downwards there was but a wooden stump upon the right side. At the sound of his strident, angry cries, there was movement in the huddled bundle upon the deck. It straightened itself into a little black man—the smallest I have even seen—with a great, misshapen head and a shock of tangled, dishevelled hair. Holmes had already drawn his revolver, and I whipped out mine at the sight of this savage, distorted creature. He was wrapped in some sort of dark ulster or blanket, which left only his face exposed ; but that face was enough to give a man a sleepless night. Never have I seen features so deeply marked with all bestiality and cruelty. His small eyes glowed and burned with a sombre light, and his thick lips were writhed back from his teeth, which

grinned and chattered at us with half animal
fury.

'Fire if he raises his hand,' said Holmes
quietly.

We were within a boat's-length by this
time, and almost within touch of our quarry.
I can see the two of them now as they stood,
the white man with his legs far apart, shriek-
ing out curses, and the unhallowed dwarf
with his hideous face, and his strong yellow
teeth gnashing at us in the light of our
lantern.

It was well that we had so clear a view of
him. Even as we looked he plucked out
from under his covering a short, round piece
of wood, like a school-ruler, and clapped it to
his lips. Our pistols rang out together. He
whirled round, threw up his arms, and, with
a kind of choking cough, fell sideways into
the stream. I caught one glimpse of his
venomous, menacing eyes amid the white

swirl of the waters. At the same moment
the wooden-legged man threw himself upon
the rudder and put it hard down, so that his
boat made straight in for the southern bank,
while we shot past her stern, only clearing
her by a few feet. We were round after her
in an instant, but she was already nearly at
the bank. It was a wild and desolate place,
where the moon glimmered upon a wide
expanse of marsh-land, with pools of stagnant
water and beds of decaying vegetation. The
launch, with a dull thud, ran up upon the
mud-bank, with her bow in the air and her
stern flush with the water. The fugitive
sprang out, but his stump instantly sank its
whole length into the sodden soil. In vain
he struggled and writhed. Not one step
could he possibly take either forwards or
backwards. He yelled in impotent rage, and
kicked frantically into the mud with his other
foot ; but his struggles only bored his wooden

pin the deeper into the sticky bank. When
we brought our launch alongside he was so
firmly anchored that it was only by throwing
the end of a rope over his shoulders that we
were able to haul him out, and to drag him,
like some evil fish, over our side. The two
Smiths, father and son, sat sullenly in their
launch, but came aboard meekly enough
when commanded. The *Aurora* herself we
hauled off and made fast to our stern. A
solid iron chest of Indian workmanship stood
upon the deck. This, there could be no
question, was the same that had contained
the ill-omened treasure of the Sholtos. There
was no key, but it was of considerable
weight, so we transferred it carefully to our
own little cabin. As we steamed slowly
up-stream again, we flashed our search-
light in every direction, but there was no
sign of the Islander. Somewhere in the
dark ooze at bottom of the Thames lie

the bones of that strange visitor to our shores.

'See here,' said Holmes, pointing to the wooden hatchway. 'We were hardly quick enough with our pistols.' There, sure enough, just behind where we had been standing, stuck one of those murderous darts which we knew so well. It must have whizzed between us at the instant we fired. Holmes smiled at it and shrugged his shoulders in his easy fashion, but I confess that it turned me sick to think of the horrible death which had passed so close to us that night.

CHAPTER XI.

THE GREAT AGRA TREASURE.

OUR captive sat in the cabin opposite to the
iron box which he had done so much and
waited so long to gain. He was a sunburned,
reckless-eyed fellow, with a network of lines
and wrinkles all over his mahogany features,
which told of a hard, open-air life. There was
a singular prominence about his bearded chin
which marked a man who was not to be
easily turned from his purpose. His age
may have been fifty or thereabouts, for his
black, curly hair was thickly shot with gray.
His face in repose was not an unpleasing
one, though his heavy brows and aggressive
chin gave him, as I had lately seen, a terrible

expression when moved to anger. He sat now with his handcuffed hands upon his lap, and his head sunk upon his breast, while he looked with his keen, twinkling eyes at the box which had been the cause of his ill-doings. It seemed to me that there was more sorrow than anger in his rigid and contained countenance. Once he looked up at me with a gleam of something like humour in his eyes.

'Well, Jonathan Small,' said Holmes, lighting a cigar, 'I am sorry that it has come to this.'

'And so am I, sir,' he answered frankly. 'I don't believe that I can swing over the job. I give you my word on the book that I never raised hand against Mr. Sholto. It was that little hell-hound Tonga who shot one of his cursed darts into him. I had no part in it, sir. I was as grieved as if it had been my blood-relation. I welted the little devil with the slack end of the rope for it, but it was done, and I could not undo it again.'

'Have a cigar,' said Holmes; 'and you had best take a pull out of my flask, for you are very wet. How could you expect so small and weak a man as this black fellow to overpower Mr. Sholto and hold him while you were climbing the rope?'

'You seem to know as much about it as if you were there, sir. The truth is that I hoped to find the room clear. I knew the habits of the house pretty well, and it was the time when Mr. Sholto usually went down to his supper. I shall make no secret of the business. The best defence that I can make is just the simple truth. Now, if it had been the old major I would have swung for him with a light heart. I would have thought no more of knifing him than of smoking this cigar. But it's cursed hard that I should be

14

lagged over this young Sholto, with whom I
had no quarrel whatever.

'You are under the charge of Mr. Athelney
Jones, of Scotland Yard. He is going to
bring you up to my rooms, and I shall ask
you for a true account of the matter. You
must make a clean breast of it, for if you do
I hope that I may be of use to you. I think
I can prove that the poison acts so quickly
that the man was dead before ever you reached
the room.'

'That he was, sir. I never got such a
turn in my life as when I saw him grinning
at me with his head on his shoulder as I
climbed through the window. It fairly shook
me, sir. I'd have half killed Tonga for it if
he had not scrambled off. That was how he
came to leave his club, and some of his darts
too, as he tells me, which I dare say helped
to put you on our track; though how you
kept on it is more than I can tell. I don't

feel no malice against you for it. But it does seem a queer thing,' he added, with a bitter smile, ' that I, who have a fair claim to half a million of money, should spend the first half of my life building a breakwater in the Andamans, and am like to spend the other half digging drains at Dartmoor. It was an evil day for me when first I clapped eyes upon the merchant Achmet and had to do with the Agra treasure, which never brought anything but a curse yet upon the man who owned it. To him it brought murder, to Major Sholto it brought fear and guilt, to me it has meant slavery for life.'

At this moment Athelney Jones thrust his broad face and heavy shoulders into the tiny cabin.

' Quite a family party,' he remarked. ' I think I shall have a pull at that flask, Holmes. Well, I think we may all congratulate each other. Pity we didn't take the other alive ;

14--2

but there was no choice. I say, Holmes, you must confess that you cut it rather fine. It was all we could do to overhaul her.'

'All is well that ends well,' said Holmes. 'But I certainly did not know that the *Aurora* was such a clipper.'

'Smith says she is one of the fastest launches on the river, and that if he had had another man to help him with the engines we should never have caught her He swears he knew nothing of this Norwood business.'

'Neither he did,' cried our prisoner—'not a word. I chose his launch because I heard that she was a flier. We told him nothing; but we paid him well, and he was to get something handsome if we reached our vessel, the *Esmeralda*, at Gravesend, outward bound for the Brazils.'

'Well, if he has done no wrong we shall see that no wrong comes to him. If we are pretty quick in catching our men, we are not so quick in condemning them.' It was amusing to notice how the consequential Jones was already beginning to give himself airs on the strength of the capture. From the slight smile which played over Sherlock Holmes's face, I could see that the speech had not been lost upon him.

' We will be at Vauxhall Bridge presently,' said Jones, ' and shall land you, Dr. Watson, with the treasure-box. I need hardly tell you that I am taking a very grave responsibility upon myself in doing this. It is most irregular ; but of course an agreement is an agreement. I must, however, as a matter of duty, send an inspector with you, since you have so valuable a charge. You will drive, no doubt ?'

' Yes, I shall drive.'

' It is a pity there is no key, that we may make an inventory first. You will have to break it open. Where is the key, my man ?'

'At the bottom of the river,' said Small shortly.

'Hum! There was no use your giving this unnecessary trouble. We have had work enough already through you. However, doctor, I need not warn you to be careful. Bring the box back with you to the Baker Street rooms. You will find us there, on our way to the station.

They landed me at Vauxhall, with my heavy iron box, and with a bluff, genial inspector as my companion. A quarter of an hour's drive brought us to Mrs. Cecil Forrester's. The servant seemed surprised at so late a visitor. Mrs. Cecil Forrester was out for the evening, she explained, and likely to be very late. Miss Morstan, however, was in the drawing-room; so to the drawing-room I went, box in hand, leaving the obliging inspector in the cab.

She was seated by the open window,

dressed in some sort of white diaphanous material, with a little touch of scarlet at the neck and waist. The soft light of a shaded lamp fell upon her as she leaned back in the basket chair, playing over her sweet grave face, and tinting with a dull, metallic sparkle the rich coils of her luxuriant hair. One white arm and hand drooped over the side of the chair, and her whole pose and figure spoke of an absorbing melancholy. At the sound of my footfall she sprang to her feet, however, and a bright flush of surprise and of pleasure coloured her pale cheeks.

'I heard a cab drive up,' she said. 'I thought that Mrs. Forrester had come back very early, but I never dreamed that it might be you. What news have you brought me?'

'I have brought something better than news,' said I, putting down the box upon the table and speaking jovially and boisterously, though my heart was heavy within me. 'I

have brought you something which is worth
all the news in the world.   I have brought
you a fortune.'

She glanced at the iron box.

' Is that the treasure then ?' she asked,
coolly enough.

' Yes, this is the great Agra treasure.
Half of it is yours and half is Thaddeus
Sholto's.   You will have a couple of hundred
thousand each.   Think of that !   An annuity
of ten thousand pounds.   There will be few
richer young ladies in England.   Is it not
glorious ?'

I think that I must have been rather over-
acting my delight, and that she detected a
hollow ring in my congratulations, for I saw
her eyebrows rise a little, and she glanced at
me curiously.

' If I have it,' said she, ' I owe it to you.'

' No, no,' I answered, ' not to me, but to
my friend Sherlock Holmes.   With all the

will in the world, I could never have followed up a clue which has taxed even his analytical genius. As it was, we very nearly lost it at the last moment.'

'Pray sit down and tell me all about it, Dr. Watson,' said she.

I narrated briefly what had occurred since I had seen her last. Holmes's new method of search, the discovery of the Aurora, the appearance of Athelney Jones, our expedition in the evening, and the wild chase down the Thames. She listened with parted lips and shining eyes to my recital of our adventures. When I spoke of the dart which had so narrowly missed us, she turned so white that I feared that she was about to faint.

'It is nothing,' she said, as I hastened to pour her out some water. 'I am all right again. It was a shock to me to hear that I had placed my friends in such horrible peril.'

'That is all over,' I answered. 'It was

nothing. I will tell you no more gloomy details. Let us turn to something brighter. There is the treasure. What could be brighter than that ? I got leave to bring it with me, thinking that it would interest you to be the first to see it.'

'It would be of the greatest interest to me,' she said. There was no eagerness in her voice, however. It had struck her, doubtless, that it might seem ungracious upon her part to be indifferent to a prize which had cost so much to win.

'What a pretty box!' she said, stooping over it. 'This is Indian work, I suppose ?'

'Yes ; it is Benares metal-work.'

'And so heavy!' she exclaimed, trying to raise it. 'The box alone must be of some value. Where is the key ?'

'Small threw it into the Thames,' I answered. 'I must borrow Mrs. Forrester's poker.'

There was in the front a thick and broad hasp, wrought in the image of a sitting Buddha. Under this I thrust the end of the poker and twisted it outward as a lever. The hasp sprang open with a loud snap. With trembling fingers I flung back the lid. We both stood gazing in astonishment. The box was empty!

No wonder that it was heavy. The iron-work was two-thirds of an inch thick all round. It was massive, well made, and solid, like a chest constructed to carry things of great price, but not one shred or crumb of metal or jewellery lay within it. It was absolutely and completely empty.

'The treasure is lost,' said Miss Morstan calmly.

As I listened to the words and realized what they meant, a great shadow seemed to pass from my soul. I did not know how this Agra treasure had weighed me down, until now that it was finally removed. It was selfish, no doubt, disloyal, wrong, but I could realize nothing save that the golden barrier was gone from between us.

'Thank God!' I ejaculated from my very heart.

She looked at me with a quick, questioning smile.

'Why do you say that?' she asked.

'Because you are within my reach again,' I said, taking her hand. She did not withdraw it. 'Because I love you, Mary, as truly as ever a man loved a woman. Because this treasure, these riches, sealed my lips. Now that they are gone I can tell you how I love you. That is why I said, "Thank God."'

'Then I say "Thank God," too,' she whispered, as I drew her to my side.

Whoever had lost a treasure, I knew that night that I had gained one.

CHAPTER XII.

THE STRANGE STORY OF JONATHAN SMALL.

A VERY patient man was that inspector in the cab, for it was a weary time before I rejoined him. His face clouded over when I showed him the empty box.

'There goes the reward!' said he gloomily. 'Where there is no money there is no pay. This night's work would have been worth a tenner each to Sam Brown and me if the treasure had been there.'

'Mr. Thaddeus Sholto is a rich man,' I said; 'he will see that you are rewarded, treasure or no.'

The inspector shook his head despondently, however.

'It's a bad job,' he repeated; 'and so Mr. Athelney Jones will think.'

His forecast proved to be correct, for the detective looked blank enough when I got to Baker Street and showed him the empty box. They had only just arrived, Holmes, the prisoner, and he, for they had changed their plans so far as to report themselves at a station upon the way. My companion lounged in his arm-chair with his usual listless expression, while Small sat stolidly opposite to him with his wooden leg cocked over his sound one. As I exhibited the empty box he leaned back in his chair and laughed aloud.

'This is your doing, Small,' said Athelney Jones angrily.

'Yes, I have put it away where you shall never lay hand upon it,' he cried exultantly. 'It is my treasure, and if I can't have the loot I'll take darned good care that no one

else does. I tell you that no living man has
any right to it, unless it is three men who are
in the Andaman convict-barracks and myself.
I know now that I cannot have the use of it,
and I know that they cannot. I have acted
all through for them as much as for myself.
It's been the sign of four with us always.
Well, I know that they would have had me
do just what I have done, and throw the
treasure into the Thames rather than let it go
to kith or kin of Sholto or Morstan. It was
not to make them rich that we did for Achmet.
You'll find the treasure where the key is, and
where little Tonga is. When I saw that
your launch must catch us, I put the loot away
in a safe place. There are no rupees for you
this journey.'

'You are deceiving us, Small,' said Athelney Jones sternly; 'if you had wished to
throw the treasure into the Thames, it would

have been easier for you to have thrown box
and all.'

'Easier for me to throw, and easier for you
to recover,' he answered, with a shrewd, side-
long look. 'The man that was clever enough
to hunt me down is clever enough to pick an
iron box from the bottom of a river. Now
that they are scattered over five miles or so,
it may be a harder job. It went to my heart
to do it, though. I was half mad when you
came up with us. However, there's no good
grieving over it. I've had ups in my life, and
I've had downs, but I've learned not to cry
over spilled milk.'

'This is a very serious matter, Small,' said
the detective. 'If you had helped justice,
instead of thwarting it in this way, you would
have had a better chance at your trial.'

'Justice!' snarled the ex-convict. 'A
pretty justice! Whose loot is this, if it is not
ours? Where is the justice that I should

give it up to those who have never earned it?
Look how I have earned it! Twenty long
years in that fever-ridden swamp, all day at
work under the mangrove-tree, all night
chained up in the filthy convict-huts, bitten by
mosquitoes, racked with ague, bullied by every
cursed black-faced policeman who loved to
take it out of a white man. That was how I
earned the Agra treasure, and you talk to me
of justice because I cannot bear to feel that I
have paid this price only that another may
enjoy it! I would rather swing a score of
times, or have one of Tonga's darts in my
hide, than live in a convict's cell and feel that
another man is at his ease in a palace with
the money that should be mine.'

Small had dropped his mask of stoicism,
and all this came out in a wild whirl of words,
while his eyes blazed and the handcuffs
clanked together with the impassioned movement of his hands. I could understand, as I

15

saw the fury and the passion of the man, that it was no groundless or unnatural terror which had possessed Major Sholto when he first learned that the injured convict was upon his track.

'You forget that we know nothing of all this,' said Holmes quietly. 'We have not heard your story, and we cannot tell how far justice may originally have been on your side.'

'Well, sir, you have been very fair-spoken to me, though I can see that I have you to thank that I have these bracelets upon my wrists. Still, I bear no grudge for that. It is all fair and above-board. If you want to hear my story, I have no wish to hold it back. What I say to you is God's truth, every word of it. Thank you, you can put the glass beside me here, and I'll put my lips to it if I am dry.

'I am a Worcestershire man myself, born

near Pershore. I dare say you would find a heap of Smalls living there now if you were to look. I have often thought of taking a look round there, but the truth is that I was never much of a credit to the family, and I doubt if they would be so very glad to see me. They were all steady, chapel-going folk, small farmers, well known and respected over the country-side, while I was always a bit of a rover. At last, however, when I was about eighteen, I gave them no more trouble, for I got into a mess over a girl, and could only get out of it again by taking the Queen's shilling and joining the 3rd Buffs, which was just starting for India.

'I wasn't destined to do much soldiering, however. I had just got past the goose-step, and learned to handle my musket, when I was fool enough to go swimming in the Ganges. Luckily for me, my company sergeant, John Holders, was in the water at

15—2

the same time, and he was one of the finest
swimmers in the service.   A crocodile took
me, just as I was half-way across, and nipped
off my right leg as clean as a surgeon could
have done it, just above the knee.   What
with the shock and the loss of blood, I
fainted, and should have been drowned if
Holder had not caught hold of me and
paddled for the bank.   I was five months in
hospital over it, and when at last I was able
to limp out of it with this timber toe strapped
to my stump, I found myself invalided out of
the army and unfitted for any active occu-
pation.

'I was, as you can imagine, pretty down
on my luck at this time, for I was a useless
cripple, though not yet in my twentieth
year.   However, my misfortune soon proved
to be a blessing in disguise.   A man named
Abel White, who had come out there as an
indigo-planter, wanted an overseer to look

after his coolies and keep them up to their
work. He happened to be a friend of our
colonel's, who had taken an interest in me
since the accident. To make a long story
short, the colonel recommended me strongly
for the post, and, as the work was mostly
to be done on horseback, my leg was no
great obstacle, for I had enough knee left
to keep a good grip on the saddle. What
I had to do was to ride over the plantation, to keep an eye on the men as they
worked, and to report the idlers. The pay
was fair, I had comfortable quarters, and
altogether I was content to spend the re-
mainder of my life in indigo-planting. Mr.
Abel White was a kind man, and he would
often drop into my little shanty and smoke
a pipe with me, for white folk out there feel
their hearts warm to each other as they
never do here at home.

'Well, I was never in luck's way long.

Suddenly, without a note of warning, the great mutiny broke upon us. One month India lay as still and peaceful, to all appearance, as Surrey or Kent; the next there were two hundred thousand black devils let loose, and the country was a perfect hell. Of course you know all about it, gentlemen —a deal more than I do, very like, since reading is not in my line. I only know what I saw with my own eyes. Our plantation was at a place called Muttra, near the border of the North-west Provinces. Night after night the whole sky was alight with the burning bungalows, and day after day we had small companies of Europeans passing through our estate with their wives and children, on their way to Agra, where were the nearest troops. Mr. Abel White was an obstinate man. He had it in his head that the affair had been exaggerated, and that it would blow over as suddenly as it had

sprung up. There he sat on his veranda,
drinking whisky-pegs and smoking cheroots,
while the country was in a blaze about him.
Of course we stuck by him, I and Dawson,
who, with his wife, used to do the book-
work and the managing. Well, one fine
day the crash came. I had been away on
a distant plantation, and was riding slowly
home in the evening, when my eye fell upon
something all huddled together at the bottom
of a steep nullah. I rode down to see what
it was, and the cold struck through my heart
when I found it was Dawson's wife, all cut
into ribbons, and half eaten by jackals and
native dogs. A little farther up the road
Dawson himself was lying on his face, quite
dead, with an empty revolver in his hand,
and four Sepoys lying across each other in
front of him. I reined up my horse, wondering which way I should turn; but at that
moment I saw thick smoke curling up from

Abel White's bungalow, and the flames beginning to burst through the roof. I knew
then that I could do my employer no good,
but would only throw my own life away if
I meddled in the matter. From where I
stood I could see hundreds of the black
fiends, with their red coats still on their
backs, dancing and howling round the burning house. Some of them pointed at me,
and a couple of bullets sang past my head :
so I broke away across the paddy-fields,
and found myself late at night safe within
the walls at Agra.

'As it proved, however, there was no
great safety there, either. The whole
country was up like a swarm of bees.
Wherever the English could collect in little
bands they held just the ground that their
guns commanded. Everywhere else they
were helpless fugitives. It was a fight of
the millions against the hundreds; and the

cruellest part of it was that these men that
we fought against, foot, horse, and gunners,
were our own picked troops, whom we
had taught and trained, handling our own
weapons and blowing our own bugle-calls.
At Agra there were the 3rd Bengal Fusiliers,
some Sikhs, two troops of horse, and a
battery of artillery. A volunteer corps of
clerks and merchants had been formed, and
this I joined, wooden leg and all. We went
out to meet the rebels at Shahgunge early in
July, and we beat them back for a time, but
our powder gave out, and we had to fall back
upon the city.

'Nothing but the worst news came to us
from every side — which is not to be
wondered at, for if you look at the map
you will see that we were right in the heart
of it. Lucknow is rather better than a
hundred miles to the east, and Cawnpore
about as far to the south. From every point

on the compass there was nothing but torture
and murder and outrage.

'The city of Agra is a great place,
swarming with fanatics and fierce devil-
worshippers of all sorts. Our handful of
men were lost among the narrow, winding
streets. Our leader moved across the river,
therefore, and took up his position in the old
fort of Agra. I don't know if any of you
gentlemen have ever read or heard anything
of that old fort. It is a very queer place
the queerest that ever I was in, and I have
been in some rum corners, too. First of all
it is enormous in size. I should think that
the enclosure must be acres and acres. There
is a modern part, which took all our garrison,
women, children, stores, and everything else,
with plenty of room over. But the modern
part is nothing like the size of the old
quarter, where nobody goes, and which is
given over to the scorpions and the centi-

pedes. It is all full of great deserted halls, and winding passages, and long corridors twisting in and out, so that it is easy enough for folk to get lost in it. For this reason it was seldom that anyone went into it, though now and again a party with torches might go exploring.

'The river washes along the front of the old fort, and so protects it, but on the sides and behind there are many doors, and these had to be guarded, of course, in the old quarter as well as in that which was actually held by our troops. We were short-handed, with hardly men enough to man the angles of the building and to serve the guns. It was impossible for us, therefore, to station a strong guard at every one of the innumerable gates. What we did was to organize a central guard-house in the middle of the fort, and to leave each gate under the charge of one white man and two or three natives. I was selected to take charge during certain hours of the night of a small isolated door upon the south-west side of the building. Two Sikh troopers were placed under my command, and I was instructed if anything went wrong to fire my musket, when I might rely upon help coming at once from the central guard. As the guard was a good two hundred paces away, however, and as the space between was cut up into a labyrinth of passages and corridors, I had great doubts as to whether they could arrive in time to be of any use in case of an actual attack.

'Well, I was pretty proud at having this small command given me, since I was a raw recruit, and a game-legged one at that. For two nights I kept the watch with my Punjaubees. They were tall, fierce-looking chaps, Mahomet Singh and Abdullah Khan by name, both old fighting men, who had

borne arms against us at Chilian Wallah.
They could talk English pretty well, but I
could get little out of them.   They preferred
to stand together and jabber all night in
their queer Sikh lingo.   For myself, I used
to stand outside the gateway, looking down
on the broad, winding river and on the twinkling lights of the great city.   The beating of
drums, the rattle of tomtoms, and the yells
and howls of the rebels, drunk with opium
and with bang, were enough to remind us
all night of our dangerous neighbours across
the stream.   Every two hours the officer of
the night used to come round to all the posts,
to make sure that all was well.

'The third night of my watch was dark
and dirty, with a small driving rain.   It was
dreary work standing in the gateway hour
after hour in such weather.   I tried again
and again to make my Sikhs talk, but without
much success.   At two in the morning the

rounds passed, and broke for a moment the
weariness of the night.   Finding that my
companions would not be led into conversation, I took out my pipe, and laid down my
musket to strike the match.   In an instant
the two Sikhs were upon me.   One of them
snatched my firelock up and levelled it at
my head, while the other held a great knife
to my throat and swore between his teeth
that he would plunge it into me if I moved
a step.

'My first thought was that these fellows
were in league with the rebels, and that this
was the beginning of an assault.   If our door
were in the hands of the Sepoys the place
must fall, and the women and children be
treated as they were in Cawnpore.   Maybe
you gentlemen think that I am just making
out a case for myself, but I give you my
word that when I thought of that, though I
felt the point of the knife at my throat, I

opened my mouth with the intention of
giving a scream, if it was my last one, which
might alarm the main guard. The man who
held me seemed to know my thoughts; for,
even as I braced myself to it, he whispered :
"Don't make a noise. The fort is safe
enough. There are no rebel dogs on this
side of the river." There was the ring of
truth in what he said, and I knew that if I
raised my voice I was a dead man. I could
read it in the fellow's brown eyes. I waited,
therefore, in silence, to see what it was that
they wanted from me.

' " Listen to me, Sahib," said the taller and
fiercer of the pair, the one whom they called
Abdullah Khan. " You must either be with
us now, or you must be silenced for ever.
The thing is too great a one for us to
hesitate. Either you are heart and soul with
us on your oath on the cross of the Christians,
or your body this night shall be thrown into

the ditch, and we shall pass over to our
brothers in the rebel army. There is no
middle way. Which is it to be—death or
life ? We can only give you three minutes
to decide, for the time is passing, and all
must be done before the rounds come
again."

'" How can I decide?" said I. "You
have not told me what you want of me. But
I tell you now that if it is anything against
the safety of the fort I will have no truck
with it, so you can drive home your knife
and welcome."

'" It is nothing against the fort," said he.
"We only ask you to do that which your
countrymen come to this land for. We ask
you to be rich. If you will be one of us this
night, we will swear to you upon the naked
knife, and by the threefold oath which no
Sikh was ever known to break, that you shall
have your fair share of the loot. A quarter of

the treasure shall be yours.   We can say no
fairer."

' " But what is the treasure, then ?" I
asked.   " I am as ready to be rich as you
can be, if you will but show me how it can
be done."

' " You will swear, then," said he, " by the
bones of your father, by the honour of your
mother, by the cross of your faith, to raise
no hand and speak no word against us,
either now or afterwards ?"

' " I will swear it," I answered, " provided
that the fort is not endangered."

' " Then my comrade and I will swear that
you shall have a quarter of the treasure which
shall be equally divided among the four of
us."

' " There are but three," said I.

' " No : Dost Akbar must have his share.
We can tell the tale to you while we wait
them.   Do you stand at the gate Mahomet

16

Singh, and give notice of their coming. The thing stands thus, Sahib, and I tell it to you because I know that an oath is binding upon a Feringhee, and that we may trust you. Had you been a lying Hindoo, though you had sworn by all the gods in their false temples, your blood would have been upon the knife and your body in the water. But the Sikh knows the Englishman, and the Englishman knows the Sikh. Hearken, then, to what I have to say.

' " There is a rajah in the northern provinces who has much wealth, though his lands are small. Much has come to him from his father, and more still he has set by himself, for he is of a low nature, and hoards his gold rather than spend it. When the troubles broke out he would be friends both with the lion and the tiger—with the Sepoy and with the Company's Raj. Soon, however, it seemed to him that the white men's day was come, for through all the land he could hear of nothing but of their death and their overthrow. Yet, being a careful man, he made such plans that, come what might, half at least of his treasure should be left to him. That which was in gold and silver he kept by him in the vaults of his palace, but the most precious stones and the choicest pearls that he had he put in an iron box, and sent it by a trusty servant, who, under the guise of a merchant, should take it to the fort at Agra, there to lie until the land is at peace. Thus, if the rebels won he would have his money, but if the Company conquered his jewels would be saved to him. Having thus divided his hoard, he threw himself into the cause of the Sepoys, since they were strong upon his borders. By his doing this, mark you, Sahib, his property becomes the due of those who have been true to their salt.

16—2

'" This pretended merchant, who travels under the name of Achmet, is now in the city of Agra, and desires to gain his way into the fort. He has with him as travelling-companion my foster-brother Dost Akbar, who knows his secret. Dost Akbar has promised this night to lead him to a side-postern of the fort, and has chosen this one for his purpose. Here he will come presently, and here he will find Mahomet Singh and myself awaiting him. The place is lonely, and none shall know of his coming. The world shall know of the merchant Achmet no more, but the great treasure of the rajah shall be divided among us. What say you to it, Sahib ?"

' In Worcestershire the life of a man seems a great and a sacred thing ; but it is very different when there is fire and blood all round you, and you have been used to meeting death at every turn. Whether Achmet the

merchant lived or died was a thing as light
as air to me, but at the talk about the treasure
my heart turned to it, and I thought of what
I might do in the old country with it, and
how my folk would stare when they saw
their ne'er-do weel coming back with his
pockets full of gold moidores. I had, therefore, already made up my mind. Abdullah
Khan, however, thinking that I hesitated,
pressed the matter more closely.

'" Consider, Sahib," said he, " that if this
man is taken by the commandant he will be
hung or shot, and his jewels taken by the
Government, so that no man will be a rupee
the better for them. Now, since we do the
taking of him, why should we not do the
rest as well ? The jewels will be as well
with us as in the Company's coffers. There
will be enough to make everyone of us rich
men and great chiefs. No one can know
about the matter, for here we are cut off from

all men. What could be better for the purpose? Say again, then, Sahib, whether you are with us, or if we must look upon you as an enemy."

'"I am with you heart and soul," said I.

'"It is well," he answered, handing me back my firelock. "You see that we trust you, for your word, like ours, is not to be broken. We have now only to wait for my brother and the merchant."

'"Does your brother know, then, of what you will do?" I asked.

'"The plan is his. He has devised it. We will go to the gate and share the watch with Mahomet Singh."

'The rain was still falling steadily, for it was just the beginning of the wet season. Brown, heavy clouds were drifting across the sky, and it was hard to see more than a stone-cast. A deep moat lay in front of our door, but the water was in places nearly dried up,

and it could easily be crossed. It was strange
to me to be standing there with those two
wild Punjaubees waiting for the man who was
coming to his death.

'Suddenly my eye caught the glint of a
shaded lantern at the other side of the moat.
It vanished among the mound-heaps, and
then appeared again coming slowly in our
direction.

'"Here they are !" I exclaimed.

'"You will challenge him, Sahib, as usual,"
whispered Abdullah. "Give him no cause for
fear. Send us in with him, and we shall do
the rest while you stay here on guard. Have
the lantern ready to uncover, that we may be
sure that it is indeed the man."

'The light had flickered onwards, now
stopping and now advancing, until I could
see two dark figures upon the other side of
the moat. I let them scramble down the
sloping bank, splash through the mire, and

climb half-way up to the gate, before I challenged them.

' "Who goes there ?" said I, in a subdued voice.

' " Friends," came the answer. I uncovered my lantern and threw a flood of light upon them. The first was an enormous Sikh, with a black beard which swept nearly down to his cummerbund. Outside of a show I have never seen so tall a man. The other was a little fat, round fellow, with a great yellow turban, and a bundle in his hand, done up in a shawl. He seemed to be all in a quiver with fear, for his hands twitched as if he had the ague, and his head kept turning to left and right with two bright little twinkling eyes, like a mouse when he ventures out from his hole. It gave me the chills to think of killing him, but I thought of the treasure, and my heart set as hard as a flint within me. When he saw my white face he gave a little

chirrup of joy, and came running up towards
me.

' "Your protection, Sahib," he panted,
"your protection for the unhappy merchant
Achmet. I have travelled across Rajpootana
that I might seek the shelter of the fort at
Agra. I have been robbed and beaten and
abused because I have been the friend of the
Company. It is a blessed night this when I
am once more in safety—I and my poor
possessions."

' " What have you in the bundle ?" I asked.

' " An iron box," he answered, "which
contains one or two little family matters which
are of no value to others, but which I should
be sorry to lose. Yet I am not a beggar;
and I shall reward you, young Sahib, and
your governor also, if he will give me the
shelter I ask."

' I could not trust myself to speak longer
with the man. The more I looked at his fat,

frightened face, the harder did it seem that we should slay him in cold blood. It was best to get it over.

' " Take him to the main guard," said I. The two Sikhs closed in upon him on each side, and the giant walked behind, while they marched in through the dark gateway. Never was a man so compassed round with death. I remained at the gateway with the lantern.

' I could hear the measured tramp of their footsteps sounding through the lonely corridors. Suddenly it ceased, and I heard voices, and a scuffle, with the sound of blows. A moment later there came, to my horror, a rush of footsteps coming in my direction, with a loud breathing of a running man. I turned my lantern down the long straight passage, and there was the fat man, running like the wind, with a smear of blood across his face, and close at his heels, bounding like a tiger,

the great black-bearded Sikh, with a knife
flashing in his hand. I have never seen a
man run so fast as that little merchant. He
was gaining on the Sikh, and I could see that
if he once passed me and got to the open air
he would save himself yet. My heart
softened to him, but again the thought of his
treasure turned me hard and bitter. I cast
my firelock between his legs as he raced past,
and he rolled twice over like a shot rabbit.
Ere he could stagger to his feet the Sikh was
upon him, and buried his knife twice in his side.
The man never uttered moan nor moved
muscle, but lay where he had fallen. I think
myself that he may have broken his neck with
the fall. You see, gentlemen, that I am
keeping my promise. I am telling you every
word of the business just exactly as it
happened, whether it is in my favour or not.'

He stopped, and held out his manacled
hands for the whisky-and-water which

Holmes had brewed for him. For myself, I confess that I had now conceived the utmost horror of the man, not only for this cold-blooded business in which he had been concerned, but even more for the somewhat flippant and careless way in which he narrated it. Whatever punishment was in store for him, I felt that he might expect no sympathy from me. Sherlock Holmes and Jones sat with their hands upon their knees, deeply interested in the story, but with the same disgust written upon their faces. He may have observed it, for there was a touch of defiance in his voice and manner as he proceeded.

'It was all very bad, no doubt,' said he. 'I should like to know how many fellows in my shoes would have refused a share of this loot when they knew that they would have their throats cut for their pains. Besides, it was my life or his when once he was in the fort. If he had got out, the whole business would come to light, and I should have been court-martialled and shot as likely as not; for people were not very lenient at a time like that.'

'Go on with your story,' said Holmes shortly.

'Well, we carried him in, Abdullah, Akbar, and I. A fine weight he was, too, for all that he was so short. Mahomet Singh was left to guard the door. We took him to a place which the Sikhs had already prepared. It was some distance off, where a winding passage leads to a great empty hall, the brick walls of which were all crumbling to pieces. The earth floor had sunk in at one place, making a natural grave, so we left Achmet the merchant there, having first covered him over with loose bricks. This done, we all went back to the treasure.

'It lay where he had dropped it when he

was first attacked. The box was the same which now lies open upon your table. A key was hung by a silken cord to that carved handle upon the top. We opened it, and the light of the lantern gleamed upon a collection of gems such as I have read of and thought about when I was a little lad at Pershore. It was blinding to look upon them. When we had feasted our eyes we took them all out and made a list of them. There were one hundred and forty-three diamonds of the first water, including one which has been called, I believe, "the Great Mogul," and is said to be the second largest stone in existence. Then there were ninety-seven very fine emeralds, and one hundred and seventy rubies, some of which, however, were small. There were forty carbuncles, two hundred and ten sapphires, sixty-one agates, and a great quantity of beryls, onyxes, cats'-eyes, turquoises, and other stones, the very names of which I did not know at the time, though I have become more familiar with them since. Besides this, there were nearly three hundred very fine pearls, twelve of which were set in a gold coronet. By the way, these last had been taken out of the chest, and were not there when I recovered it.

'After we had counted our treasures we put them back into the chest and carried them to the gateway to show them to Mahomet Singh. Then we solemnly re-newed our oath to stand by each other and be true to our secret. We agreed to conceal our loot in a safe place until the country should be at peace again, and then to divide it equally among ourselves. There was no use dividing it at present, for if gems of such value were found upon us it would cause suspicion, and there was no privacy in the fort nor any place where we could keep them. We carried the box, therefore, into the same hall where we had buried the body, and there, under certain bricks in the best-preserved wall, we made a hollow and put our treasure. We made careful note of the place, and next day I drew four plans, one for each of us, and put the sign of the four of us at the bottom, for we had sworn that we should each always act for all, so that none might take advantage. That is an oath that I can put my hand to my heart and swear that I have never broken.

'Well, there's no use my telling you gentlemen what came of the Indian mutiny. After Wilson took Delhi and Sir Colin relieved Lucknow the back of the business was broken. Fresh troops came pouring in, and Nana Sahib made himself scarce over the frontier. A flying column under Colonel Greathed came round to Agra and cleared the Pandies away from it. Peace seemed to be settling upon the country, and we four were beginning to hope that the time was at hand when we might safely go off with our shares of the plunder. In a moment, however, our hopes were shattered by our being arrested as the murderers of Achmet.

It came about in this way. When the rajah put his jewels into the hands of Achmet he did it because he knew that he was a trusty man. They are suspicious folk in the East, however : so what does this rajah do but take a second even more trusty servant and set him to play the spy upon the first ? This second man was ordered never to let Achmet out of his sight, and he followed him like his shadow. He went after him that night, and saw him pass through the doorway. Of course he thought he had taken refuge in the fort, and applied for admission there himself next day, but could find no trace of Achmet. This seemed to him so strange that he spoke about it to a sergeant

17

of guides, who brought it to the ears of the commandant. A thorough search was quickly made, and the body was discovered. Thus at the very moment that we thought that all was safe we were all four seized and brought to trial on a charge of murder—three of us because we had held the gate that night, and the fourth because he was known to have been in the company of the murdered man Not a word about the jewels came out at the trial, for the rajah had been deposed and driven out of India : so no one had any particular interest in them. The murder, however, was clearly made out, and it was certain that we must all have been concerned in it. The three Sikhs got penal servitude for life, and I was condemned to death, though my sentence was aftewards commuted into the same as the others.

' It was rather a queer position that we found ourselves in then. There we were all four tied by the leg and with precious little chance of ever getting out again, while we each held a secret which might have put each of us in a palace if we could only have made use of it. It was enough to make a man eat his heart out to have to stand the kick and the cuff of every petty jack-in-office, to have rice to eat and water to drink, when that gorgeous fortune was ready for him outside, just waiting to be picked up. It might have driven me mad; but I was always a pretty stubborn one, so I just held on and bided my time.

'At last it seemed to me to have come. I was changed from Agra to Madras, and from there to Blair Island in the Andamans. There are very few white convicts at this settlement, and, as I had behaved well from the first, I soon found myself a sort of privileged person. I was given a hut in Hope Town, which is a small place on the slopes of

17—2

Mount Harriet, and I was left pretty much to myself. It is a dreary, fever-stricken place, and all beyond our little clearings was infested with wild cannibal natives, who were ready enough to blow a poisoned dart at us if they saw a chance. There was digging and ditching and yam-planting, and a dozen other things to be done, so we were busy enough all day; though in the evening we had a little time to ourselves. Among other things, I learned to dispense drugs for the surgeon, and picked up a smattering of his knowledge. All the time I was on the look-out for a chance of escape; but it is hundreds of miles from any other land, and there is little or no wind in those seas: so it was a terribly difficult job to get away.

'The surgeon, Dr. Somerton, was a fast, sporting young chap, and the other young officers would meet in his rooms of an evening and play cards. The surgery, where I used to make up my drugs, was next to his sitting-room, with a small window between us. Often, if I felt lonesome, I used to turn out the lamp in the surgery, and then, standing there, I could hear their talk and watch their play. I am fond of a hand at cards myself, and it was almost as good as having one to watch the others. There was Major Sholto, Captain Morstan, and Lieutenant Bromley Brown, who were in command of the native troops, and there was the surgeon himself, and two or three prison-officials, crafty old hands who played a nice sly safe game. A very snug little party they used to make.

' Well, there was one thing which very soon struck me, and that was that the soldiers used always to lose and the civilians to win. Mind, I don't say there was anything unfair, but so it was. These prison-chaps had done little else than play cards ever since they had been at the Andamans, and they knew each other's game to a point, while the others just played to pass the time and threw their cards down anyhow. Night after night the soldiers got up poorer men, and the poorer they got the more keen they were to play. Major Sholto was the hardest hit. He used to pay in notes and gold at first, but soon it came to notes of hand and for big sums. He sometimes would win for a few deals, just to give him heart, and then the luck would set in against him worse than ever. All day he would wander about as black as thunder, and he took to drinking a deal more than was good for him.

' One night he lost even more heavily than usual. I was sitting in my hut when he and Captain Morstan came stumbling along on the way to their quarters. They were bosom friends, those two, and never far apart. The Major was raving about his losses.

'"It's all up, Morstan," he was saying, as they passed my hut. "I shall have to send in my papers. I am a ruined man."

'"Nonsense, old chap!" said the other, slapping him upon the shoulder. "I've had a nasty facer myself, but——" That was all I could hear, but it was enough to set me thinking.

'A couple of days later Major Sholto was strolling on the beach: so I took the chance of speaking to him.

'"I wish to have your advice, Major," said I.

'"Well, Small, what is it?" he asked, taking his cheroot from his lips.

'"I wanted to ask you, sir," said I, "who is the proper person to whom hidden treasure should be handed over   I know where half a million worth lies, and, as I cannot use it myself, I thought perhaps the best thing that I could do would be to hand it over to the proper authorities, and then perhaps they would get my sentence shortened for me."

' "Half a million, Small?" he gasped, looking hard at me to see if I was in earnest.

' "Quite that, sir—in jewels and pearls. It lies there ready for anyone. And the queer thing about it is that the real owner is outlawed and cannot hold property, so that it belongs to the first comer."

' " To Government, Small," he stammered, " to Government." But he said it in a halting fashion, and I knew in my heart that I had got him.

' " You think, then, sir, that I should give the information to the Governor-General?" said I quietly.

' "Well, well, you must not do anything rash, or that you might repent. Let me hear all about it, Small. Give me the facts."

' I told him the whole story, with small changes, so that he could not identify the places. When I had finished he stood stock still and full of thought. I could see by the twitch of his lip that there was a struggle going on within him.

' "This is a very important matter, Small," he said at last. "You must not say a word to anyone about it, and I shall see you again soon."

'Two nights later he and his friend, Captain Morstan, came to my hut in the dead of the night with a lantern.

' "I want you just to let Captain Morstan hear that story from your own lips, Small," said he.

'I repeated it as I had told it before.

' "It rings true, eh?" said he. " It's good enough to act upon?"

'Captain Morstan nodded.

' "Look here, Small," said the Major. "We have been talking it over, my friend here and I, and we have come to the conclusion that this secret of yours is hardly a Government matter, after all, but is a private concern of your own, which of course you have the power of disposing of as you think best. Now the question is, What price would you ask for it? We might be inclined to take it up, and at least look into it, if we could agree as to terms." He tried to speak in a cool, careless way, but his eyes were shining with excitement and greed.

' "Why, as to that, gentlemen," I answered, trying also to be cool, but feeling as excited as he did, "there is only one bargain which a man in my position can make. I shall want you to help me to my freedom, and to help my three companions to theirs. We shall then take you into partnership, and give you a fifth share to divide between you."

' "Hum !" said he. "A fifth share ! That is not very tempting."

' " It would come to fifty thousand apiece," said I.

' " But how can we gain your freedom ? You know very well that you ask an impossibility."

' " Nothing of the sort," I answered. " I have thought it all out to the last detail. The only bar to our escape is that we can get no boat fit for the voyage, and no provisions to last us for so long a time. There are plenty of little yachts and yawls at Calcutta or Madras which would serve our turn well. Do you bring one over. We shall engage to get aboard her by night, and if you will drop us on any part of the Indian coast you will have done your part of the bargain."

' " If there were only one," he said.

' " None or all," I answered. " We have sworn it. The four of us must always act together."

' " You see, Morstan," said he, " Small is a

man of his word.   He does not flinch from his friends.   I think we may very well trust him."

' " It's a dirty business," the other answered.   " Yet, as you say, the money will save our commissions handsomely."

' " Well, Small," said the Major, " we must, I suppose, try and meet you.   We must first, of course, test the truth of your story.   Tell me where the box is hid, and I shall get leave of absence and go back to India in the monthly relief-boat to inquire into the affair."

' " Not so fast," said I, growing colder as he got hot.   " I must have the consent of my three comrades.   I tell you that it is four or none with us."

' " Nonsense !" he broke in.   " What have three black fellows to do with our agreement ?"

' " Black or blue," said I, "they are in with me, and we all go together."

'Well, the matter ended by a second meeting, at which Mahomet Singh, Abdullah
Khan, and Dost Akbar were all present.
We talked the matter over again, and at last
we came to an arrangement. We were to
provide both the officers with charts of the
part of the Agra fort, and mark the place in
the wall where the treasure was hid. Major
Sholto was to go to India to test our story.
If he found the box he was to leave it there,
to send out a small yacht provisioned for a
voyage, which was to lie off Rutland Island,
and to which we were to make our way, and
finally to return to his duties. Captain
Morstan was then to apply for leave of
absence, to meet us at Agra, and there we
were to have a final division of the treasure,
he taking the Major's share as well as his
own. All this we sealed by the most solemn
oaths that the mind could think or the lips
utter. I sat up all night with paper and ink,

and by the morning I had the two charts
all ready, signed with the sign of four—
that is, of Abdullah, Akbar, Mahomet, and
myself.

'Well, gentlemen, I weary you with my
long story, and I know that my friend Mr.
Jones is impatient to get me safely stowed in
chokey. I'll make it as short as I can. The
villain Sholto went off to India, but he never
came back again. Captain Morstan showed
me his name among a list of passengers in
one of the mail-boats very shortly afterwards.
His uncle had died, leaving him a fortune,
and he had left the army ; yet he could stoop
to treat five men as he had treated us.
Morstan went over to Agra shortly afterwards, and found, as we expected, that the
treasure was indeed gone. The scoundrel
had stolen it all, without carrying out one
of the conditions on which we had sold him
the secret. From that day I lived only for

vengeance. I though of it by day and I nursed it by night. It became an over-powering, absorbing passion with me. I cared nothing for the law—nothing for the gallows. To escape, to track down Sholto, to have my hand upon his throat—that was my one thought. Even the Agra treasure had come to be a smaller thing in my mind than the slaying of Sholto.

'Well, I have set my mind on many things in this life, and never one which I did not carry out. But it was weary years before my time came. I have told you that I had picked up something of medicine. One day when Dr. Somerton was down with a fever a little Andaman Islander was picked up by a convict-gang in the woods. He was sick to death, and had gone to a lonely place to die. I took him in hand, though he was as venomous as a young snake, and after a couple of months I got

him all right and able to walk. He took
a kind of fancy to me then, and would
hardly go back to his woods, but was always
hanging about my hut. I learned   little
of his lingo from him, and this made him
all the fonder of me.

'Tonga—for that was his name—was a
fine boatman, and owned a big, roomy canoe
of his own. When I found that he was
devoted to me and would do anything to
serve me, I saw my chance of escape. I
talked it over with him. He was to bring
his boat round on a certain night to an old
wharf which was never guarded, and there
he was to pick me up. I gave him directions
to have several gourds of water and a lot of
yams, cocoa-nuts, and sweet potatoes.

'He was stanch and true, was little Tonga.
No man ever had a more faithful mate. At
the night named he had his boat at the
wharf. As it chanced, however, there was

one of the convict-guard down there—a vile
Pathan who had never missed a chance of
insulting and injuring me. I had always
vowed vengeance, and now I had my chance.
It was as if fate had placed him in my way
that I might pay my debt before I left the
island. He stood on the bank with his back
to me, and his carbine on his shoulder. I
looked about for a stone to beat out his
brains with, but none could I see.

'Then a queer thought came into my
head, and showed me where I could lay my
hand on a weapon. I sat down in the darkness and unstrapped my wooden leg. With
three long hops I was on him. He put his
carbine to his shoulder, but I struck him
full, and knocked the whole front of his
skull in. You can see the split in the wood
now where I hit him. We both went down
together, for I could not keep my balance;
but when I got up I found him still lying

18

quiet enough. I made for the boat, and in
an hour we were well out at sea. Tonga
had brought all his earthly possessions with
him, his arms and his gods. Among other
things, he had a long bamboo spear, and
some Andaman cocoa-nut matting, with
which I made a sort of a sail. For ten
days we were beating about, trusting to
luck, and on the eleventh we were picked
up by a trader which was going from
Singapore to Jiddah with a cargo of Malay
pilgrims. They were a rum crowd, and
Tonga and I soon managed to settle down
among them. They had one very good
quality : they let you alone and asked no
questions.

'Well, if I were to tell you all the adventures that my little chum and I went through,
you would not thank me, for I would have
you here until the sun was shining. Here
and there we drifted about the world, some-

thing always turning up to keep us from London. All the time, however, I never lost sight of my purpose. I would dream of Sholto at night. A hundred times I have killed him in my sleep. At last, however, some three or four years ago, we found ourselves in England. I had no great difficulty in finding where Sholto lived, and I set to work to discover whether he had realized the treasure, or if he still had it. I made friends with someone who could help me—I name no names, for I don't want to get anyone else in a hole—and I soon found that he still had the jewels. Then I tried to get at him in many ways; but he was pretty sly, and had always two prize-fighters, besides his sons and his khitmutgar, on guard over him.

'One day, however, I got word that he was dying. I hurried at once to the garden, mad that he should slip out of my clutches like that, and, looking through the window,

18—2

I saw him lying in his bed, with his sons on each side of him. I'd have come through and taken my chance with the three of them, only even as I looked at him his jaw dropped, and I knew that he was gone. I got into his room that same night, though, and I searched his papers to see if there was any record of where he had hidden our jewels. There was not a line, however, so I came away, bitter and savage as a man could be. Before I left I bethought me that if I ever met my Sikh friends again it would be a satisfaction to know that I had left some mark of our hatred; so I scrawled down the sign of the four of us, as it had been on the chart, and I pinned it on his bosom. It was too much that he should be taken to the grave without some token from the men whom he had robbed and befooled.

'We earned a living at this time by my exhibiting poor Tonga at fairs and other such

places as the black cannibal. He would eat
raw meat and dance his war-dance: so we
always had a hatful of pennies after a day's
work. I still heard all the news from Pondicherry Lodge, and for some years there was
no news to hear, except that they were hunt-
ing for the treasure. At last, however, came
what we had waited for so long. The
treasure had been found. It was up at the
top of the house, in Mr. Bartholomew Sholto's
chemical laboratory. I came at once and
had a look at the place, but I could not see
how, with my wooden leg, I was to make my
way up to it. I learned, however, about a
trap-door in the roof, and also about Mr.
Sholto's supper-hour. It seemed to me that
I could manage the thing easily through
Tonga. I brought him out with me with a
long rope wound round his waist. He could
climb like a cat, and he soon made his way
through the roof, but, as ill luck would have

it, Bartholomew Sholto was still in the room, to his cost. Tonga thought he had done something very clever in killing him, for when I came up by the rope I found him strutting about as proud as a peacock. Very much surprised was he when I made at him with the rope's end and cursed him for a little bloodthirsty imp. I took the treasure box and let it down, and then slid down myself, having first left the sign of the four upon the table, to show that the jewels had come back at last to those who had most right to them. Tonga then pulled up the rope, closed the window, and made off the way that he had come.

' don't know that I have anything else to tell you. I had heard a waterman speak of the speed of Smith's launch, the *Aurora*, so I thought she would be a handy craft for our escape. I engaged with old Smith, and was to give him a big sum if he got us safe to our ship. He knew, no doubt, that there was some screw loose but he was not in our secrets. All this is the truth, and if I tell it to you, gentlemen, it is not to amuse you—for you have not done me a very good turn—but it is because I believe the best defence I can make is just to hold back nothing, but let all the world know how badly I have myself been served by Major Sholto, and how innocent I am of the death of his son.'

'A very remarkable account,' said Sherlock Holmes. 'A fitting wind-up to an extremely interesting case. There is nothing at all new to me in the latter part of your narrative, except that you brought your own rope. That I did not know. By the way, I had hoped that Tonga had lost all his darts; yet he managed to shoot one at us in the boat.'

'He had lost them all, sir, except the one which was in his blow-pipe at the time.'

' Ah, of course,' said Holmes.   ' I had not thought of that.'

' Is there any other point which you would like to ask about ?' asked the convict affably.

'I think not, thank you,' my companion answered.

' Well, Holmes,' said Athelney Jones, ' you are a man to be humoured, and we all know that you are a connoisseur of crime ; but duty is duty, and I have gone rather far in doing what you and your friend asked me.   I shall feel more at ease when we have our story-teller here safe under lock and key.   The cab still waits, and there are two inspectors down-stairs.   I am much obliged to you both for your assistance.   Of course you will be wanted at the trial.   Good-night to you.'

'Good-night, gentlemen both,' said Jonathan Small.

' You first, Small,' remarked the wary Jones as they left the room.   ' I'll take particular care that you don't club me with your wooden leg, whatever you may have done to the gentleman at the Andaman Isles.'

'Well, and there is the end of our little drama,' I remarked, after we had sat some time smoking in silence. 'I fear that it may be the last investigation in which I shall have the chance of studying your methods. Miss Morstan has done me the honour to accept me as a husband in prospective.'

He gave a most dismal groan.

'I feared as much,' said he. 'I really cannot congratulate you.'

I was a little hurt.

'Have you any reason to be dissatisfied with my choice ?' I asked.

'Not at all. I think she is one of the most charming young ladies I ever met, and might have been most useful in such work as we have been doing. She had a decided genius that way; witness the way in which she preserved that Agra plan from all the other papers of her father. But love is an emotional thing, and whatever is emotional is opposed to that true cold reason which I place above all things. I should never marry myself, lest I bias my judgment.'

'I trust,' said I, laughing, 'that my judgment may survive the ordeal. But you look weary.'

'Yes, the reaction is already upon me. I shall be as limp as a rag for a week.'

'Strange,' said I, 'how terms of what in another man I should call laziness alternate with your fits of splendid energy and vigour.'

'Yes,' he answered, 'there are in me the makings of a very fine loafer, and also of a pretty spry sort of a fellow. I often think of those lines of old Goethe:

'Schade dass die Natur nur *einen* Mensch aus dir schuf,
Denn zum würdigen Mann war und zum Schelmen der Stoff.'

By the way, *à propos* of this Norwood business, you see that they had, as I surmised, a confederate in the house, who could be none other than Lal Rao, the butler: so Jones actually has the undivided honour of having caught one fish in his great haul.'

'The division seems rather unfair,' I remarked. 'You have done all the work in this business. I get a wife out of it, Jones gets the credit, pray what remains for you?'

'For me,' said Sherlock Holmes, 'there still remains the cocaine-bottle.' And he stretched his long white hand up for it.

THE END.